Annie Thomas

Walter Goring

a story - Vol. 3

Annie Thomas

Walter Goring
a story - Vol. 3

ISBN/EAN: 9783337391881

Printed in Europe, USA, Canada, Australia, Japan

Cover: Foto ©Andreas Hilbeck / pixelio.de

More available books at **www.hansebooks.com**

WALTER GORING.

𝕬 𝔖𝔱𝔬𝔯𝔶.

BY

ANNIE THOMAS,

AUTHOR OF "DENIS DONNE," "ON GUARD," "THEO LEIGH," ETC.

"And yet, believe me, good as well as ill,
Woman's at best a contradiction still."

IN THREE VOLUMES.

VOL. III.

LONDON:

CHAPMAN & HALL, 193, PICCADILLY.

1866.

LONDON:
BRADBURY, EVANS, AND CO,, PRINTERS, WHITEFRIARS.

CONTENTS.

WALTER GORING.

CHAPTER I.

LOVE'S YOUNG DREAM.

WALTER GORING knew that Daisy was wayward and wilful; but at the same time—despite those little tricks of hers—he did believe her to be the truest, purest, tenderest child, in whom a man ever trusted. He recalled all her endearing ways— the shimmer of her dear blue eyes—the pouting of the red wet mouth, that was always so ready to kiss him. He recalled all these, as the train whirled him down to Brighton the following day, and altogether thought himself round into a very tender frame of mind about Daisy. Moreover, he was additionally tender to her, in consequence of a vague and indistinct feeling he had, of having been more wrought upon by other women lately than Daisy would altogether have approved of, could she have

known it. He thought that the dear loving child
who had given him the first fruits of her heart
deserved this at least in return, namely, that no
lingering old romance should ever disturb him
again.

Nor should it do so. There was pain, un-
doubtedly—pleasurable pain, perhaps, but still pain
in the lately-gained knowledge that Mrs. Walsh
loved him. It was utterly impossible that any
man should have been indifferent to the love of such
a woman. It was such gloriously gratifying love,
too—it was so utterly unselfish, as strong and generous at what she had declared to be "the last," as
when it might have been repaid. For all his good
intentions as to maintaining perfect· fidelity of
thought even to Daisy, his mind would dwell a
good deal on the last words and the possible future
of her who had been his goddess.

Not that he would have exchanged Daisy for her
now. Before his engagement, had he been certain
of that of which he was now certain about Mrs.
Walsh, Daisy would have lost the game which she
came down to play. But he, not being certain of
it, had gone on suffering the probability·to remain
in the haze it had been only discreet to suffer it

to remain in for so many years. Warm friendship had been all that he dared to suppose she felt for him in the past; so he had continued to take the warm friendship for granted till it was too late.

Not too late for his happiness: that would be well assured he hoped, and nearly felt convinced, in a marriage with Daisy—the true-hearted, if occasionally wrong-headed. Not too late for his happiness, but too late for " hers," he half thought, and then checked himself for being a conceited coxcomb; and told himself that Mrs. Walsh would in all probability love and marry one of the many men who worshipped her from afar.

An awful twinge of unadulterated jealousy shot through his heart as the probability struck him: " I hope not; it would drive me mad to see her married to any fellow who didn't appreciate her; it's quite enough to see that poor girl down at Deneham—to have another woman I admire and esteem in such a position would be too much."

The heart is deceitful above all things and desperately wicked; or rather, the simultaneous birth of a dozen emotions, each one good in itself, and their consequent clashing, frequently makes it appear so. On the whole, Walter Goring was not sorry when the train stopped at Brighton and he was forced into action. It might have been an interesting study to analyse his own conduct and feelings, and the mainsprings of both; but assuredly it would have been a painful and humiliating one.

He meant this visit to be an unexpected treat to Daisy, and he was quite sensible enough to feel that it was worth while to try and appear at his very best, before the girl who was now bound to him. So he sent round to the stables where Daisy's horse was kept, and had the chestnut saddled; and when he was dressed he rode out to Mrs. Osborne's villa, looking, as Daisy observed from an upstairs window, a splendid specimen of a modern cavalier. The small trouble he had taken was not thrown away. With a woman's quickness of perception on these, and indeed most points, Daisy marked in a glance the daintiness of all the accessories of his costume: the trim cut and careful arrangement of his brown hair and golden-brown beard,—the perfection of each detail that goes to the making-up of a well-bred man's morning-dress. She marked it all, and felt proud that he was her lover, and hoped that several people would see him, and know that she

was a much more important person than his ward—
that she was going to be his wife. Then she heard
from the servant that Mrs. and Miss Osborne were
both out, and she reflected that since none were by
to see him, it would have been just as well for him
to have come later. "I wonder how long he'll
stay?" she thought, as she slowly dressed herself;
" if he will go out for a walk it will be all very well;
but to sit in all the rest of the day will be dreadfully
dull and tiring."

Her eyes looked heavy, and her cheeks were very
pale and thin. She saw that they were so when
she was ready to go down at last (with what different
feelings had Horatia Walsh prepared to see him
the day before), and she tried to brighten up, and
attempted to rub a little colour into her face by
pressing her hands almost roughly over it. But it
was of no avail, so she went down at last with a
slow heavy step and a heavier heart.

There was not the faintest excitement to her in
the prospect of seeing him, whom she had lured on
to love her so tenderly. She liked him very much,
and she tried to get up a faint pleasure at this
devotion of his, by saying to herself as she went
along, " Dear Walter, how good of him to come to

me;" but she could not help adding, "I wonder what he wants, and how long he will stay?"

She made a great effort, as she neared the door, to throw off that appearance of weariness which could but strike him harshly, she knew, contrasting it, as he surely would, with her old manner before he was won. "If they had only been in to have made a fuss, it would have been all right," she thought, discontentedly; "but what's the good of his being here, when there is no one to see how fond he is of me. I hope he'll go on the pier; he's such good style that every one will look, and it will soon get about that he's *my* property." Then she opened the door, and as he came towards her holding out his arms, she sprang into them and hid her face on his waistcoat, which at once satisfied him that she was delighted to meet him, and saved her the trouble of looking so.

Presently he put his hand under her chin and raised her face, "My darling Daisy, how pale you have grown—it was time for me to come and look after you."

The shimmer he had longed to see and thought of so lovingly, came over the cobalt-blue eyes; in an instant she threw herself into her proper part.

"Think how long it is since I have seen you, Walter—and you all the time taken up with those Fellowes's."

He bent his head and kissed her on the mouth till her face flooded with crimson; and she jerked her head back sharply. "You take away my breath, Walter," she said, petulantly. "Are you going to stay here to dinner?"

"Yes, if Mrs. Osborne will give me a dinner," he replied, laughing. Then Daisy seated herself on a couch, spreading her dress over as wide an extent of it on either side as she could, and Walter lounged over the arm of it, and took up a tress of her straw-coloured hair and kissed it.

"You, Daisy," he said presently, reproachfully, "are you not going to give me one kiss when I have come so far to get it?"

She turned to him, exclaiming, "Dear Walter!" with effusion, and holding out the pouting mouth; but she took it away again in a hurry, thinking, "Oh, dear! if this is to go on for hours what a bother it will be."

"Shall I sing to you, Walter, dear?" she asked.

"No, speak to me, my pet." If any one had been by to see him then as he came before her and clasped her round the waist, Daisy would have been delighted. As it was, though she began putting his hair further off his forehead with her old bewitching touch, she was thinking, "I wish he wasn't so spoony—it tires me out."

"I have nothing to speak about, Walter. I am so desperately dull here."

"Then I have something to speak about. I want you to promise me something, Daisy, darling."

A frightened look came into her eyes.

"Oh, it's not about *that*, is it, Walter?"

"What?"

"What I won't tell."

"No, dearest. I want you to promise me that you will be my wife in May: it's sooner than we thought of at first, but it will be better for many reasons. Will you have me in May, Daisy?"

For a few moments her bosom heaved convulsively, and her mouth quivered. Then she recovered herself and laughed.

"Yes, on the first of May, Walter, if you like."

"The dear unconventional Daisy," he thought, fondly; "most girls would have humbugged about it."

"And now let me sing to you," she said, hastily, when he had thanked her with another kiss, and she had undulated away from under it.

"My darling, you can sing to me when other people are here," he pleaded.

She checked a resigned sigh which she had been about to heave, and looked as if she thought his suggestion a delightful amendment on her own. Then he took out the diamond and emerald bracelet; and Daisy put it on, and gave way to ecstasies of admiration. When she had done, he framed a neat little message from Mrs. Walsh for her; but he omitted that statement Mrs. Walsh had made relative to Daisy "shining her down."

"They're lovely," Daisy said, and she meant all she said about them. "Oh, Walter, they make one feel bright and sparkling, don't they? I'd like some for my neck and some for my head."

"You shall have them, dear; they shall be one of my presents to you on our wedding-day: the other is to be a picture, in which Mrs. Walsh figures."

"Yes. I heard of that when I was with Mrs. Fellowes. Has her brother found a— whoever it was he wanted to find, yet?"

"A model for 'Elaine.' Yes; I haven't seen it, though we went to his studio yesterday on purpose. St. John was out, unfortunately."

St. John's being out was indeed unfortunate— far more unfortunate than poor Walter Goring had any idea of.

"Whom do you mean by 'we'?" Daisy asked, quickly, with the carping jealousy that springs from vanity, not love.

"I walked up with Mrs. Walsh."

"Walter, I believe you are very fond of Mrs. Walsh?"

"I know I am," he answered.

"And I believe she's in love with you," she continued.

"Then you believe what is not true."

"Do you mean to say that she is not, Walter?"

"I mean to say that any man who thought it, would be a blind fool not to test the truth of his thought; and I am not that, Daisy."

A queer expression—half sorrowful, half satiric— shot from her eyes as he spoke. She seemed to be pondering over his words for a few moments; then she replied—

"So, if you had thought that she was in love with

you, you would have proposed to her instead of to me; isn't that what you mean?"

"Yes," he answered, resolutely, "I would; for in that case I should have been in love with her. As it was, you see, none of these conditions were fulfilled. You won me instead, and will never have reason to be jealous of anything I have felt, or might have felt, or may feel for another woman."

"No; I will never be jealous, Walter. I hope you won't either?"

"I won't promise that," he said, laughing.

She heaved a short full sigh.

"You will never have cause. I shall not be a married flirt, like your friends, Mrs. Walsh and Mrs. Fellowes. I believe Mrs. Fellowes likes you much better than she does her husband, which isn't to be wondered at."

"You believe most extraordinary things," he said, more gravely than he had yet spoken. "I'm afraid you have studied human nature in a bad school, dear."

She shook her head vehemently.

"I have indeed," she said, bitterly. "Oh, Walter, do forgive me! I ought not to forget what my parents were when I am talking in this way."

"Daisy, dearest, your over-sensitiveness makes you unnatural. Don't speak—don't think of your parents in such a way. Remember one is dead, and the other is ——"

"Worse," she interrupted hastily. "Well, if you won't let me sing to you, Walter, come out for a walk on the pier?"

"I hate the pier. I'll go for a walk anywhere else with you."

"On the parade?"

"That's as bad as the pier. Let us go along this road, it looks quiet and pretty enough."

"It's so dull," she said, pettishly. She wanted to take him out and show him, in order that those acquaintances whom she had made through the Osbornes might see him, and say what a fine young man Miss Goring was engaged to. There would have been a little pleasurable excitement in such a walk; but there would be none in going along a dull road, where no one would mark and inquire about him, and find out that, in addition to being a fine young man, he was the owner of a fine property, a cele- brated novelist, and her own very devoted slave.

"I would just as soon stay in, dear," she said softly.

"And I would much rather stay in," he replied. And again Daisy began to feel terribly bored.

Perhaps if she could have known of those two recent scenes, and the sensations which beset the female actors in them—the spirit of emulation, the feeling of pride, which is said to be engendered in the feminine breast when the fact of winning a man who has been wanted by other women is made patent, would have come to the aid of the fatigued Daisy, and caused her to feel the time less tedious. As it was, she could hardly help yawning. She was bored; and he was so all-potent with such much better women. It was a mis-shapen order of things unquestionably.

"I tell you what, Daisy," he said, after a time; "I shall take you to Rome to see the Levinges."

She shrugged her shoulders. "Did I ever tell you about Mary Levinge coming here?" she asked, with what she would not suffer to be a blush.

"Coming here?"

"Yes. She wanted me to go and stay with them in Rome."

"Mary Levinge must have had some reason for such an extraordinary proceeding," he said, meditatively. Then he asked abruptly, "What was it, Daisy?"

"I don't know. Caprice, I suppose. They liked me; and was there anything so very extraordinary in *that?*"

"My pet, everyone likes you" (with a magnificent disregard of truth); "but everyone does not invite you to stay with them in this way. What brought it about, Daisy?"

"I'm sure I don't know. Go and make your Mary Levinge account for her own caprice. Don't come to me for an explanation," she said, hotly, tossing the straw-coloured head. "You think all she does is proper, and all she says is right; she has unsexed herself."

"Daisy, that's not your own sentiment; that is one of her graceless brother's."

"Oh! *don't* make me give up my authority for every word I use, Walter. If you begin that, I shall be afraid to speak before you." Then she laughed, and put her arms round his neck, and added—

"You're so accustomed to plagiarise yourself, you mean boy, that you can't help suspecting me of doing the same. Do try to believe that I think Miss Levinge rather coarse all out of my own head."

"Mary Levinge never does anything without a motive," he replied, seriously.

"What a disagreeable toad she must be to be always planning. Well, I will find a motive for this, and flatter your vanity. She wanted to get me out of your way; they are *all* in love with you, Walter, and you think more highly of every one of them (the deceitful wretches) than you do of me."

"You remarkably unjust and illogical Daisy," he said, laughing; "you foolish jealous pet,"—it was quite pleasant to him to imagine that she was jealous—he rather cultivated the idea. "Do you think that Mary Levinge and I nurse a hopeless passion for each other?"

"I don't suppose you would ever have a hopeless passion for such a great big-handed woman," Daisy replied. "What she may do for you I can't say."

"There being no accounting for taste, hers may be as bad as your own, you think?" he replied, laughing. On which she got up and said,—

"Now I will sit down and sing, Walter; you get so dreadfully silly."

She sang to him without cessation, until Mrs. Osborne and Alice came in. She sang to him, and at him, and amused herself very well, and he looked upon all the vocal efforts as so many pure and simple-minded attempts to please him still further. He was very much in love with her youth and delicacy. The way in which she shrank from his passion whenever it became demonstrative allured him; she was " Warning the touch while winning the sense, and charming most when she most repelled," in a very pleasing way, considering she was to be his wife. After all, as he told himself that night when he rode back into Brighton, his was the happiest choice—the freshest selection. Those other women, for all their subtle charms, had loved others, even if they had unloved again! But Daisy! Daisy was the driven snow; the softest, richest bloom rested still undisturbed upon the peach he was going to pick. She was all his own! there was no old ro-mance to dispute possession of her heart with him. Heaven shone in her dear blue eyes for him, and— he never dreamt that he was in a fool's paradise.

CHAPTER II.

"WOMAN'S AT BEST A CONTRADICTION STILL."

LATE into the night following that unfortunate day of the auction at The Hurst, young Mrs. Fellowes sat on a little stool by the fire, with her elbows on her knees, and her chin in her hands, thinking. There was no external interruption to her quiet. Her husband was lying on the sofa in a deep heavy motionless slumber, and his mother and sister had gone to bed at nine, rather tired, and more than rather huffed.

So she sat there thinking—with no fear of his speaking to her, or of their coming in. Her past life spread itself out like a panorama before her, and she went over it inch by inch as it were, courageously, though the travelling was not pleasant.

First, she recalled the old joyous reign of misrule in her father's house; the happy careless time when all her most strongly marked and worst qualities had been encouraged and applauded with admiring laughs, and· with an affected censure that was a still more flattering form of admiration. Her frank defiant nature—her restless spirit—her intense passion for all that was new—her habit of impatience—her disregard of every form of authority—her blithe contempt, too openly expressed, for all that seemed contemptible to her keen young mind ! All these qualities had been fostered by injudicious training, until they had dominated her entirely, and had caused her to domineer over others. Then her father had died, and she had learnt a portion of the bitter lesson the world is always so beautifully ready to teach those whose circumstances are altered.

She had learnt a portion of this lesson, but she had learnt it very insufficiently. It remained for Robert Prescott to impress it more fully upon her mind. If he taught her nothing else, he taught her to feel the helplessness and the humiliation of her position—and to hate it. So she escaped from it at the first opportunity; because she was too impatient to endure it, and too proud to stoop to try to amend it. She had told herself that the

situation was unendurable, therefore she never
attempted to endure. For the sake of attaining
ease and freedom, position and wealth; above all,
for the sake of attaining greater bodily and mental
independence, she had married without love, without the faintest feeling that could even have misled
herself into the idea that she did love. Never for
an instant had she deceived herself. She had told
herself that she should surely come to regard her
husband warmly, and to esteem him well; she had
vowed to be the truest friend, the most cordial
sympathiser, the most earnest and devoted adhe-
rent to the cause of the man she had married. But
she knew that she should never love him, so she
never lied about it, even to herself.

Now she was shaken to her soul as she thought
this, but still she did think it—he had dashed those
determinations of hers with doubt. Already he had
made it very hard for her to keep to the plain
path—unlighted by love—of duty. Already, he had
made it very hard; what if he should go on and
make it impossible?

She dropped her arms on her lap, and raised her
head as her thoughts reached this point, and looked
at him and—loathed him. At any sacrifice, which

could have been made wholly and solely by herself—which could never have touched or pained
another—she would have taken her freedom, and
got away somewhere—anywhere; away out of the
possibility of ever seeing him again as he was. If
she could have concentrated all the pain and dis-
honour and anxiety on herself—if the very few
who loved her would never have felt a pang—she
thought that she would not have cared into what
outer darkness she might flee, so long as she
escaped from this house of bondage. But she
knew that she could not so concentrate the pain
and anxiety, and she could not shake the faith
those had in her, who by believing her to be so
good, had made her better.

"No, it must be borne," she thought, placing her
face down into her hands again. But how? It
must be borne, together with the knowledge so
startlingly brought home to her heart this day, that
a man whom she could have loved, knew how to
soothe, and fire, and value her.

It was a dangerous knowledge. She knew that it
was dangerous, and at first she tried to check the
remembrance she had of it, and of the manner in
which the knowledge had been gained. But this

putting aside a thing, was foreign to her nature. There was something mean, not to say cowardly in it. "I may as well face the facts," she thought, with a little shake of the head. " I behaved disgracefully this afternoon—any man with a grain of feeling would have done what he did, when I cried at him, and put my hand on his arm; it has made all things ten times harder to bear than they would have been without it, and that's a fitting punishment for me; but there will always be the feeling and the memory, and what *am* I to do with them."

She rose up as she thought this, and went over with soft steps to look at her husband, who had slept on through this storm that was raging in his wife—slept on, not in blest, but in brutal unconsciousness. There would always be this in addition to the feeling and memory of that which had gained form and substance in that brief moment when Walter Goring lost his head—this—this man, who was losing the power to guard her honour and his own—this man, who was already a thing to blush and tremble for, and shrink from.

She began to sicken at the thought of his awakening—he would be so fearfully ashamed and penitent,

and how could she respond? "I really hope he
will not say a word," she thought. "I hope he
will never look me in the face again; what a life
mine is. I have to turn away from something on
every side; why couldn't he have left me something to hold on by? now I have nothing; where
shall I drift?"

Once more she sat down, and with a little
groan, went on "thinking out" the subject after
the manner of women. It was hard, very, very hard.
But she sat up erect under the sudden conviction
—she was not the sole, or indeed the most important consideration in this business. What if
she felt his—her husband's—degradation? would
he not feel it himself ten times more? What if
she regretted a vanished possibility, a moment's
weakness, was there not one who would regret it
too—for her sake? Ay! and regret it in exact
proportion as she showed that she remembered it.
"I'll try and make Mr. Goring forget it all, by
seeming to forget it myself; we ought not to be
interested in each other, and he won't be so interested in me if he thinks me quite happy." Then
she felt that even if she could not be happy herself,
she might try to make others so; and she rose up

again, and with even softer steps than before, went over and re-arranged the disordered pillow under her husband's heavy head. So "she took up the burden of life again, saying only, it might have been." After all, hers was a sound, sweet nature. She had a thousand impulses in those hours of trial, but the only ones on which she acted were good. She came out of this sharpest ordeal to which she had yet been subjected intact, even if not purified and refined. But that feeling, that the burden must be taken up again after a dream of " what might have been," is almost maddening—let it come to whom it will.

Very few things come up to the expectation formed of them. The thing has been said ten thousand times in ten thousand different ways. Anticipation is invariably fairer or fouler than reality. We all know that this must be. We accept this hideous fact when we grow old; but when we are young the constant recurrence of the truth is simply overwhelming.

Charlie—poor, imaginative, faulty Charlie—made a dozen little mental sketches of what would be said and what would be looked when her husband came back to his place in the scale of humanity

again. She grew more gentle and more humble,
and so more tolerant to his faults and less tolerant
to her own every minute. Her heart throbbed as
she resolved to stem down the torrent of his self-
reproaches, and be that best of friends to him—a
friend who could wisely ignore, and cheer instead
of depressing. She felt capable of putting herself
and her own feelings out of court altogether, as she
renewed her vow of making the best of things, and
reminded herself afresh that it behoved her to
brighten, to the best of her ability, the lot of the
man who had fallen upon evil days, but who had
sought her when the sun was on him.

Her nerves were strung up now to a terrible
tension. Women of her order always go off at a
hard gallop when their burden has been readjusted.
What with her penitence and her pity, and her profound conviction that she had been guilty of the
very grossest error a delicate-minded woman can
commit in her own eyes, she was quite ready to put
herself in the position of the offender instead of the
offended when Henry Fellowes woke. For many
hours she had been dwelling with keen pain upon
the possible results of his conduct—upon the
effect it might have upon her practice, and the

effect it must have upon her character. She had been investing the occasion with very great importance. I will not say with undue importance, because that which shocks and disgusts a woman nearly out of all sense of propriety, cannot be too seriously regarded. She had looked upon it as a turning point in her destiny; it was a never-to-be-forgotten episode: and the part she meant to remember was not his short-coming, but her own. She shook all over when she saw him rousing himself; she longed to throw herself before him, and entreat him to believe that she would forget as entirely as she had already forgiven. But just as she was about to put her design in execution he got up, and stopped her, by saying,

"I think I have been asleep, Charlie; do let us get to bed at once."

Then she shrank back cold and chilled, as, I suppose, it is the just fate of those foolish ones to be, who are born with the weak habit of dying of roses in aromatic pain.

Her legs trembled under her as she walked up the creaking stairs before him. She had suffered the first moment of his recovery to pass without speaking to him, and now she could not bring herself to utter a word. She had fancied that he had looked at her angrily, and she had fancied rightly; it had not been all such utter oblivion with him as she had imagined. He had seen and felt two or three things dimly through the mists which obscured his brain, and he was aggrieved.

"Why wouldn't you come and kiss me when I asked you to do it, Charlie?" he said to her as soon as they reached their own room; "it was hard just at the time when everything is gone from me to see my wife turn away from me and go off with another man."

He put his hands on her shoulder as he spoke, and made her face him, and she stood with her head thrown back as far from him as she could.

"I couldn't do it," she replied; "if you don't know the reason I can't tell it to you."

"It stabbed me to the heart to see you rush after Goring in that way," he went on, complainingly; and when he said that she shook herself free from his detaining hands.

"I should have rushed after a dog that was leaving me alone with you then," she exclaimed in a quick low tone.

"And he consoled you, I suppose—consoled you for having a husband, who is such a poor creature that he feels it when all his old friends give him the cold shoulder," his voice broke with a sob; but he recovered, and went on immediately, "by heaven, Goring shall not play that game here."

The last part of the sentence was injudicious; she had softened when he spoke of old friends giving him the cold shoulder; but the allusion to Walter Goring stung her.

"Leave his name out of the question."

"But I won't leave his name out of the question; I'll have no man coming here supplanting me with my wife, and showing her what a much finer fellow he would be under the circumstances. I'll have no sneaking hound——"

"*Will* you stop?" she asked.

"Yes; when I have finished. It was a mean thing—a mean thing of any fellow to do. You both thought me senseless, I suppose, because I was sleepy."

"Why will you force me to remember what you were?" she asked, contemptuously.

"I daresay Goring took care to impress what I was upon you."

" You are mad."

She walked towards the door as she spoke. As she opened it he went after her, and laid his hand on her arm.

" Charlie, where are you going ? "

"Downstairs; let me go—let me go. I'm afraid to stay here to-night."

" Afraid of *me ?* "

" No, of myself." She was speaking the truth; she was terribly afraid that she might say or do something which could never be unsaid or undone. The barrier between them was quite high enough already.

"What do you want?—tell me what you want."

" I want nothing but to be let go," and as she said it, she twitched her arm away from under his hand.

" I'll have no nonsense of the kind;" he put his arm round her, and drew her back almost roughly into the room, locking the door as he did so. " The mischief has gone farther than I thought; fallen as *you* fancy me, madam, I'll show you that I am strong enough to put a stop to the puling romance of that fellow." Her strength was weakness when he said that, all her good resolutions failed, and she was nearly shaken to pieces by the storm of fury that swept across her soul.

"If you degrade me by acting as you say you will, I'll leave you."

"Desert me in my difficulties," he almost whined.

"Oh! if you only knew what I would have done for you, and how cheerfully I would have shared whatever troubles you have," she exclaimed, as the tide of fury ebbed again; "but how can I hope to make you understand that when you misunderstand the best friend you have."

"Meaning Walter Goring?" he asked.

"Yes; meaning Walter Goring," she replied, and her voice thrilled as she named him.

"Well; I want no more of his friendship," Henry Fellowes said sullenly. His head was aching violently by this time, and he was uncomfortably conscious of several things. Amongst others that the ache served him right—that he had not been absolutely victorious in this first matrimonial tussle—and that he had to get up early the following morning to ride round another man's land. After all there was much to be urged in extenuation of what he had said, and what he had done; and so Charlie came to feel when he left off talking to her, and she was free to reason and reproach herself again.

The following day she heard that the Prescotts would be down almost immediately, and that Walter Goring had gone to Brighton ; and she told herself that "it was better far that he should go than stay," and hoped that she might not see him again until after his marriage.

CHAPTER III.

THE dulness and monotony of both feeling and action which set in in the Fellowes's household after that first unfortunate quarrel between Charlie and her husband, was broken after a few weeks by an active annoyance. The Prescotts came down, and notified their arrival very shortly to Charlie in a message requesting her to go up and see her sister the following morning.

They were sitting at dinner when the message was delivered, and it told on each member of the party at once. The words "John has come down from The Hurst to say, &c." were hardly out of the servant's mouth before Henry Fellowes lost his appetite, and laid down his knife and fork. John had been one of his own grooms. The Hurst had been the home of the Felloweses for generations.

Charlie saw and sympathised with his emotion, but
it was no use increasing it by noticing it just then.
So she said—

"Give my love to Mrs. Prescott, and say I'll be
up with her in the morning."

"I think, considering all things, that Mrs. Prescott might have had the good feeling to call on us
first," old Mrs. Fellowes exclaimed, as soon as they
were alone.

"Ellen never does consider all things," Charlie
replied, good-humouredly. She was still in Mrs.
Fellowes's black books for having kept Henry to
herself on the night of the auction. The exacting
mother little knew how willingly her son would
have been released then and for ever by that young
jealously-watched detaining power.

"More shame for her, then," the old lady replied,
tartly; on which Miss Dinah remarked—

"Just so; but it's not Mrs. Henry's fault."

Charlie felt grateful to Miss Dinah. It was not
active partisanship or even zealous partisanship;
but young Mrs. Fellowes did not, therefore, think
the less of it. Indeed, on the whole she rather
preferred that which resembled the violet—that
which was just felt in the atmosphere, and not too

plainly seen. Active and zealous partisans take high rank in the army of friends from whom we pray to be delivered.

"Perhaps you will walk over with me," she suggested. "I can hardly fancy Ellen in a half-empty house arranging things."

"Oh, your sister has come to every comfort, every comfort," Mrs. Fellowes said seriously, as if there were something impious and to be regretted in the fact. "I am sure I only hope that it may last. *I* don't wish them ill. Furniture sent down from London *days* before the family arrive, and men sent down to arrange it! I hope it may last."

Charlie did not echo the expression of this hope, partly because she dared not do it, and partly because it did seem to her a matter of very small moment whether Mr. Prescott's new goods and chattels "lasted" or not. She was conscious, too, of a faint feeling of pleasure in the prospect of having her sister near her for a time. Ellen, though not a too congenial, would be a safe and tender-hearted companion, and she clung now to what was safe and kind. There had been danger in the sympathetic interest which had been the offspring of too congenial a mind; and there was utter bankruptcy at home. Every bill she had drawn of late had been dishonoured. These things conspired to make her glad even of the prospect of Ellen's society, and desirous of keeping the peace, and so enjoying that society without verbal molestation.

That conjugal scene of the unfortunate auction day had been repeated several times with variations. Mr. Fellowes, who in the days of his prosperity had seemed to be as strong-headed as he was soft-hearted, was becoming surely and, alas! not very slowly, a sorrow and spirit-sodden man. Charlie thought that it was the pecuniary ruin which had befallen him which preyed upon him, and this roused her contempt. But she wronged him there. Had she known the truth, her anger and contempt would have deepened. He had taken in a vague jealousy of his friend and distrust of his wife, and under the influence of these feelings he went a very good way to give himself cause for both, had the nature he was blindly striving to alter been worse than it was.

After that one outburst of feeling when he had made the miserable mistake of charging Walter

Goring and herself with playing a double part—a dubious game—Charlie had accepted the situation, and bravely, if not cheerfully, made the best of it. "It would have been better for us both if you had not spoken as you did last night, Henry," she said to him the following morning; "but since you have said so much, I must say a little more. You said you would not have Mr. Goring come here again. Even if you hadn't said it, I should."

"Why so?" he asked.

"Why, because I should get fond of him, probably," she replied, recklessly. "Stop, don't say a word; he'd despise me as much for it as you would, and I have a greater respect for his opinion than for that of any other human being. How should it be otherwise?—ask yourself."

She was no hypocrite, therefore she told all that there was to tell about herself. But on the other hand, she was no traitor, therefore she said no word relative to Walter Goring's share in the matter. To her own heart she acknowledged that the man had been indiscreet, but quick upon that acknowledgment followed her heart's free, eager confession to itself that she had been the cause of that indiscretion. Any blame that might fall upon herself

alone she could bear and brave; but she would
have cut her tongue out rather than utter a word
that should inculpate him. With rash truthful
recklessness she told out the tale of her being
ready to love; but with a woman's reticence she
held back the statement of another being ready
to love her, since it must injure him.

Having made a clean breast of it, she seemed
even to Henry Fellowes's jealous observation to
forget her avowal and the subject of it altogether.
As she had been a cipher at The Hurst, so she was
a cipher in the new household; but the small part
that was assigned to her she accepted and played
out bravely and contentedly. He could find no
fault with her. Her round of duties was not large,
certainly, but she never left one of them unfulfilled.
She bore with the petty details of domestic life
which his mother and sister insisted upon wearying
her with, patiently. She devoted her energies to
serving him, in every way in which it came within
the scope of her power to serve him, assiduously as
ever. She cleared up what he confused frequently.
She never suffered him to forget an appointment of
which she had once heard. With the spasmodic
energy that was one of her most prominent charac-

teristics, she got up hard dry details connected with
the management of land and property of a similar
nature to that of which her husband was now
steward, and arranged facts and successful experi-
ments and promising schemes, in such a way as
enabled him to grasp and act upon them often.
Her mind and her memory were invaluable to him,
and were always ready at his call, and yet—what
was it? He felt that, had they been in different
hemispheres, they could not have been more widely
asunder than they were; and she felt the same,
only far more keenly and remorsefully. She never
reproached him, though cause was not wanting.
She never recoiled from him outwardly. She
carried herself so contentedly, that her "pluck"
became the theme of a hymn of praise which was
constantly being chanted in her husband's ears.
But he would willingly have bartered away all
these for one love-glance from the quiet. eyes whose
language was a mystery to him—for one fond touch
from the little hand that was as unwearied in his
service as it was unwilling to meet his. But these
would never be his now—never, never! He strove
to drown his knowledge of the fact, and the drowning it made the fact itself more fatally certain.

However, externally all things were fair, that is to say, they were as fair as things ever are in a household where the means are small, and the members not united by any very strong bond of love. On second thoughts, I am far from feeling that the latter condition makes the slightest difference, so I will amend the phrase. Things were as fair as a person who had nothing to gain and little to lose, and who was yet resolved to hold on by that which was, could make them.

Before Charlie went up to The Hurst to see her sister according to promise, she received a note from Frank :—

"My dear Charlie," (he wrote) : "Your book is announced, in two volumes. I have been through the proofs for you. I think it will do very well, but don't be down-hearted even if it should not. A letter from Goring puts to flight my intention of trying to get 'Elaine' into the Academy. He wants to have it to give to his cousin the day they're married, which is to be in May, he tells me. I saw Prescott yesterday in a shooting-coat and a wideawake ; the sight was pleasant. He was just off to The Hurst, he told me. I'll send you any notices that may appear of your book, and be down soon to see how you are all getting on.

> "Your affectionate brother,
>
> "FRANK."

This letter gave her plenty to think about as she walked up to The Hurst. It afforded her pleasant —yes, of course it was pleasant, though confusing just at first—matter of reflection. Her book out, and Walter Goring to be married in May! Delightful brace of facts.

"I wish we had gone to Australia," she sighed, as she went into the house, and was immediately fallen upon by all the young Prescotts. Then she walked into what had been the drab dull drawing-room, and found it strangely metamorphosed. But Ellen was sitting there, and the sight of her, cool, and calm, and pinkily pretty as ever, did much towards reconciling incongruities.

"I'm glad you have come so early, dear," Mrs. Prescott said, as she met her sister. "I wouldn't decide on the curtains for the bedrooms till you came; you have such taste."

"My taste is at your service. Don't say by-and-by, though, when Robert makes long lips about

the bills, that you would have had the cheaper
things if it hadn't been for me. I remember the
ire and scorn I brought upon myself by exercising
my taste when you were remodelling your Bays-
water drawing-room. How pretty all this is," she
continued, looking round the room. "The difference between this room now and the first time I
saw it ! "

"Yes, it is pretty,—I must drive you home after
luncheon and see your house,—I dare say it is
pretty too, though small," Ellen replied, with the
pretentious feeble magnanimity of her order.

Charlie laughed. "I think I will leave you to
form an unbiassed judgment, Ellen ; come and
show me all the rooms, will you ? "

Mrs. Prescott was auspicious, so they went together from room to room, Charlie taking as hearty
an interest in, and expressing as unfeigned an admiration for, the improvements and alterations as
though this place had never been her own. At last
it occurred to Mrs. Prescott to say—

"I hope you don't mind it, Charlie ? "

"Mind what ? Why, I'm delighted."

"I mean, I hope you don't feel my being here, in
what was your home once."

" Indeed, no, Ellen," she said, sincerely : she had so much more to weigh her heart down and cloud her happiness, than the loss of what had never been dear to her.

" I was afraid you might;—oh, dear, what an unfortunate thing that marriage has been for you, Charlie. What a lottery marriage is, isn't it ? "

"I seem to have heard the remark before," Charlie replied, trying to laugh carelessly, but catching her breath, and nearly choking in the attempt. " At any rate, Ellen, *we've drawn*,—there is nothing more to be said."

"No, nothing ; and, as Robert says, if it has been bad for you, it has been good for us. We wanted a house in the country, and this suits us charmingly;—it's an ill wind that blows nobody any good."

" Exactly so ; let those words be the last requiem sung over the grave of my dead fortunes, dear. What a joyous time this is for the children, there's no one to look after them ; how well Ella looks ; she'll be as pretty as her mother." So she ran on until she had succeeded in luring Mrs. Prescott's thoughts entirely away from the too suggestive subject of her own marriage and its consequences.

At luncheon, Mr. Prescott appeared, looking very country-gentlemanly in his shooting-coat. It was the first garment of the sort into which he had ever inducted himself, and he was very conscious of it. He could not help giving Charlie a dubious deprecatory glance when he met her; her eyes danced and the corners of her mouth went up. " I shouldn't wonder if that brother of hers has sent her a stupid caricature of me in this costume already," he thought. " I saw him laugh. Both these young people are much too fond of laughing for their position in life."

He told his sister-in-law that he should get her husband to look out for a riding-horse for him. " A nice nag, steady, with a good spirit, one that will take me along over anything," he said, jauntily, forgetting the ditch and the brown hunter.

" I'm sure he will do it with pleasure; and I hope that you'll keep a riding-horse for Ellen, and then when she doesn't want it she'll lend it to me; won't you, dear ? "

Mr. and Mrs. Prescott both looked pleased. Charlie was so thoroughly at her ease, so entirely resigned to the inferior position, so enchantingly willing to accept the goods they and the gods gave her. Mr. Prescott loved to patronise people when he could do it inexpensively. Charlie's manner developed this love of patronage now.

"Of course she will lend it to you," he said, pompously; "in fact, any little pleasures that we *can* put in your way we *shall* put in your way."

"You're very good," she replied. She was not heeding either the matter or the manner of his speech; she was thinking of that event which was to come off in May; and hoping that they would be happier than she herself was.

"We shall entertain a good deal," Mr. Prescott went on in an expansive manner. "We shall entertain a good deal—and I may say in a good way—and we shall always expect to see you."

"And in that way you will get asked out by other people who will meet you here," Ellen struck in, in the lavishly explanatory manner.

"Get what?" Charlie interrupted.

"Asked out—invited to parties, you know."

Charlie began to laugh, then she checked herself, reflecting that it was hopeless trying to make them understand why the prospect they were seeking to open to her seemed absurd. They were meaning well, and she was so much more alive to,

and grateful for, anything that was kindly meant,
than she had been when we knew her first.   They
would think her envious and soured, perhaps, if she
explained to them that under all the circumstances
there was more pleasure to her in absolute solitude
than in any number of little evening parties.   They
would think her soured, whereas it was only her
perfect appreciation of the expediency and propriety, nay more, of the absolute necessity, of the
give-and-take system of society which dictated the
feeling.   So she checked her laugh, and asked
Robert Prescott another small favour on the spot,
in order that he might not think her ungrateful for
his more lofty and glorious designs in her behalf.

"Give me a lot of flowers to take home with me
to-day, Robert, will you?"

"Of course," Ellen replied.   "How dull you
must be, often, Charlie."

"Not often; I manage to get a good deal of time
quite to myself," Charlie replied, unguardedly.

Robert Prescott looked up at her sharply.

"A good deal of time quite to themselves is what
most young wives would consider very dull work,"
he said more gently than he had ever spoken to her
in his life before.   The touch of truth in her tone

had gone home to him. He felt at once that all was not as well even as outsiders supposed in this marriage which she had made; and his conscience, though it did not pinch him severely by any means, told him why she had made it. She blushed as he spoke, and when he paused and looked at her for an answer, she said—

"I never was romantic, you know, Robert; my own is the only society of which I should never tire, I believe." Then for the sake of appearances she attempted an equivocation, and added, "and as my husband is compelled to be away from me a great deal, I nurse the feeling as much as possible in order to keep contented."

In about a month after this, Frank fulfilled his promise of sending her all the notices that had appeared of her first venture on the literary ocean. The book itself had come down before, and had been carefully read by each member of both families; but remarks upon it in each case, save Robert Prescott's, had been reserved. Mr. Prescott, Charlie heard through Ellen, disapproved of her having published under her maiden name.

"It seems to me that that concerns Frank more than it does Robert, and Frank advised it," Charlie argued. "Never mind about that. What does Robert think of the book?"

"Well, he thinks it has some merit—some, you know."

This, though it could not come under the head of rash encouragement, was more than Charlie had expected. She was so nervously alive to the blemishes in it herself, that the merit had no opportunity of making itself apparent to her.

The first review that came down was of the laudatory order. It dealt in gorgeous prognostications of future success, and full-bodied epithets expressive of admiration. She thought it meant fame and fortune as she read it—fame and fortune, and a rapid rush up Parnassus. She learnt every word of that first review by heart, and adored the writer of it as such a discriminating demi-god deserved to be adored. Then her husband read it, and was pleased also; and then it was perused by old Mrs. Fellowes, who forthwith fell into sympathetic ecstasies, and expressed herself as coinciding entirely with the reviewer's sentiments. "And in your next, my dear, I hope you won't be ashamed to appear under your real name," she said, affably. To which Miss Dinah replied, "Perhaps

it will be just as well that she shouldn't, mother,—
you wouldn't like it if the next were a failure." In
a cooler moment Charlie would have felt all the rea-
sonableness of Miss Dinah's remark; but what
young author ever was reasonable over a first
favourable notice? Failure! after all those brilliant qualities which the intelligent reviewer had
discovered in her? The idea was too preposterously
absurd.

The following day a much more important paper
—one of the literary journals—came down, and with
it a line from Frank.

"You're well slated in the —— ; but never mind,
it's so splendidly done, you'll enjoy it," he wrote;
and thus prepared, Charlie opened the paper, and
prepared to enjoy it.

No doubt it was very enjoyable, if she could only
have gone to the perusal in a proper frame of mind.
The sentences scintillated before her eyes. The
article abounded in clever epigrams and brilliantly-
turned sentences. Nevertheless, she was very far
from enjoying the reading. Unfortunately, too, she
had opened the paper before the whole family, and
she knew that they were watching her, and felt that
she could not keep on reading and holding her

peace about it for ever. The splendour of the way
in which it was written was less visible to her
than the fact that she was denounced as " coarse "
in it. If it could have been been kept to herself
altogether, she could have accepted it as a whole-
some lesson, for she acknowledged that it only told
the truth, though it told it somewhat severely. But
she could not keep it to herself; she was only a
woman, and she knew that it would be made to
adorn morals and point endless tales for some time
to come. Even Frank, instead of being indignant
at it, thought it "splendidly done."

She gave it up reluctantly at length, and tried to
go on eating her breakfast, as if she were a callous
and time-hardened author, to whom these things
were but as the buzzing of summer insects. But
the bread went into dangerous crumbs, and the tea
seemed to scald her, when Mrs. Fellowes, who had
insisted on reading it aloud, began to shake her
head, and otherwise deplore.

But if the review itself was hard to bear, the
commentaries on it were worse.

"' Coarse!' Ah, that's what I thought, to tell the
truth," Mrs. Fellowes began. Though if she had
told the truth, she would have confessed that the

idea had never entered into her mind until she saw it there in print.

"I was afraid you had touched on one or two points that you had better have let alone, Charlie," her husband said, rather severely. "If you remember, I said so."

"Never to me, Henry."

"Oh! didn't I; well, I thought so, then." Then he ran his eye over it again when his mother put it down; and when he had finished, he said, in the tone of one who has just made a fresh and before unthought-of unpleasant discovery, "Besides, there is scarcely any plot, and no moral whatever."

"They are not 'besides' all the sins the review mentions, Henry; they are included in it, in the very words you use."

He did not look in the least ashamed of himself. Self-elected private critics are the most hardened plagiarists. He simply said, "Oh! are they? that proves me right, then." Then Dinah picked it up, and read it slowly, syllable by syllable, and Charlie steadied herself in expectation of a shock from that quarter—but it did not come. All Dinah said was, "It seems to me that if you're all going to be wafted about by every wind of doctrine in this way, that your novel-writing will be more pain than pleasure or profit to you, Mrs. Henry. There's a great deal of truth in this; but I suppose you knew that before, though neither Henry nor my mother did?"

"I've thought it all along, Dinah," the old lady replied, with dignity—"all along; it's exactly what I've thought—exactly."

"You fancy now that you have thought so, mother, that's all," Dinah replied, decidedly; and Charlie felt more grateful to her sister-in-law than ever.

She could not help wondering what Walter Goring would think of it. It would have cut her to the heart to think that he could believe her to be several things that that review implied. She hated her novel lying there in its violet binding, as she thought of this possibility. She hated her " Gerty Grey," and wished with all her heart that she could crush the fatal longing that possessed her to go on writing. But she had another nearly ready, and she could not bring herself to destroy it, or to leave it unfinished.

In the course of that morning, Mr. Prescott and Ellen came up; and just as their carriage stopped at the door, Henry Fellowes came home; so they all went into Charlie's drawing-room together, and the review was brought forth for them to look at.

When Mr. Prescott had got about half through it, he looked up at the luckless authoress, and said,—

" Well, I thought at least you would have had a good word here. Your friend, Mr. Walter Goring, does nearly all the notices of novels for this paper."

" I wish mine had fallen into his hands—he wouldn't have been so hard on it," she said, with a quickly flushing face.

" But I think—indeed, I'm almost sure—that this is his," Mr. Prescott replied, resuming his reading. " Oh, yes ; there's no doubt of it. There's a sort of tolerant taking-both-sides-of-the-question style about it that is essentially Goring's."

" H'm ! that's what you've got from your friend," Mr. Fellowes remarked, with as near an approach to sarcasm as he was capable of.

" Oh, it's Goring's, undoubtedly," Mr. Prescott pursued, with quiet satisfaction. " Know his phrases very well."

" I don't believe for one instant that it is Mr. Goring's," Charlie said, attempting to speak calmly, and falling far short of her attempt.

"You don't think that he would see a fault in you, I suppose?" her husband suggested.

"Yes, I do. Do you imagine that I think him such an idiot? Of course he would see and censure a dozen faults—but in a different way. I should be sorry, indeed, to think that any man who knew me wrote that."

"Especially Mr. Goring?" Mr. Fellowes asked.

"Especially Mr. Goring," Charlie replied, with the hardihood of desperation. Then as the remote possibility of this stab being dealt to her by Walter Goring struck her, she added, "He *couldn't* hurt me so."

"I'm sorry to shatter your faith in him," Mr. Prescott said, with a little laugh ("they were not his corns that were trodden on," and our latest lost great humourist told the truth about the consoling power of this fact, as he did about every other on which he touched),—"I'm sorry to shatter your faith in him; but there's conclusive evidence in this review, to me, that it's written by Goring. We called to take you for a drive—will you come, Charlie?"

'No, I don't think I will to-day," she said. "I had made up my mind to ask my husband to let me walk round the farm this afternoon with him; will you, Henry?"

He agreed to her proposal; and so the Prescotts went away, and the Felloweses went for a long, dull, tiring walk together. But she courted bodily fatigue this day; any amount of it was better than the thought that would intrude while she was inactive. The thought that Walter Goring thought so meanly of her as to try to cure her by cruelty! "It can't be his," she told herself a thousand times; and speedily after that telling came the miserable doubt, "Why did he do it? Walter Goring, for his own sake, ought to think better things of me than are implied in that."

So it went on rankling—that one review. No matter what the others said, for good or ill; that one which might be impregnated with his ideas about her was all in all—the thing worth living for, and living down.

CHAPTER IV.

BY THE LITTLE BROOK.

MAY was approaching rapidly, as May or any other month has a habit of approaching when something that is not regarded with rapturous impatience is to occur in it. All things were going on much as usual with the different characters of this little drama. Walter Goring was dividing his time pretty equally between Paris and Brighton. Fate kept him away from London, therefore he never chanced to see Frank St. John's picture, which was progressing steadily, and the young artist hoped and believed favourably; and something else, perhaps it was feeling, had kept him away hitherto from the vicinity of Deneham.

As for Charlie, she was, so to say, steeped in the last section of her new novel and some disquieting speculations. The dream of fame and fortune was gone, but the desire of having some interest independent of her home life still flourished. Indeed, it became more desirable every day almost that she should possess some such safeguard. Her legal lord had lost the hold he had had over her at one time; she stood by herself now, and the worst of it was that she knew that she stood by herself. As she had never had love, so now she had neither respect nor sympathy for him; nothing but pity, more than slightly dashed with contempt. In fact, she stood on shifting sands, and knew well that there was none who could help her to maintain her footing save herself.

And she was desperately afraid of failing herself. She was not one of those women who from custom and conceit believe themselves to be founded on a rock. She recognised fully and gratefully, that great truth, which so many women persist in ignoring, that her daily prayer had been answered, namely, and that she never had been " led into temptation." It is easy and pleasing to sit in the seat of the scornful over those who have not been " delivered from evil," in time to recover breath and save themselves, until one's own strength has been tried and found weakness.

Her strongest safeguard was this—that she knew many of her own worst points. She was not one of those who, because they never have done wrong, think it impossible that they ever should do wrong. She always remembered that better ones than herself had gone down in the contest to which she had never been called. Better equipped and better endowed ones had gone down—women who had far more to lose and many more weapons of defence, and who must have had originally as strong a desire as she had now to stand. The reflection inevitably induced speculation on those subjects which it is perhaps just as well that a woman should not speculate on too freely, predestination and free-will. If the former be implicitly believed in, the inutility of any effort to avert or control becomes the leading idea, and an active-minded woman is in danger of drifting into any madness that presents itself. While, on the other hand, illimitable faith in the freedom of the will does away with the cherished feminine notion of spontaneous passion, and insists upon reason ruling without a moment's cessation. Theoretically, Charlie gave in her adhesion to this form of faith; it was a creed that appealed to all that was strongest in her nature. She had a great sense of expediency, a keen sense of humour, and a profound appreciation of that power which is the portion of those alone whose heads govern their hearts. The rule of reason ranked high above the law of love in her estimation, whenever she thought about it. But for all that, she knew very well that there had been little reason and less expediency in the way in which she had suffered the warmest regard she was capable of feeling to go out and settle upon Walter Goring. Had her will been perfectly free, she would not have given herself up for one moment to his caresses. Had she believed in predestination, she would not have put a stop to them when she did. In practice, she had wavered between the two beliefs, and both had failed her; and the memory of that failure mocked her whenever she was thinking of the future and vowing always to be true to herself let what would come.

It is perhaps because we are not taught to think coherently on any topic that it is not habitual to discuss in family council or society, that directly a woman takes to thinking about anything she is almost sure to build up some frail and faulty fabric of philosophy about it. There are so many things that come before our eyes, and the mysterious mention of which falls upon our ears daily almost, that we are forbidden to " speak about," and advised not to "think about." Naturally we do think about them, but cloudily, and from the reprehending side alone. Under these circumstances, it is inevitable that either a merciless or a maudlin judgment is formed; we are either too pitiless or too pitiful. If we accept unhesitatingly the dicta of those who have discreetly thrown the halo of mystery, the charm of something to be found out, over the subject on which they recommend silence to be held, and thought to be banished, we are hardened against the offender, without having the faintest notion in what way we may be lured to the offence ourselves. While if we do not accept this view of the case, we blindly go over to exactly the opposite side, and sympathise stupidly with the result, equally without any know-ledge of the cause. Checked thought, repressed doubt, murdered misgivings, surely these have been the rule too long. To deny what is, and to believe what is not—to avow that that is impossible which is proved a possibility daily—to hope that founda-tions which are rotten will be good enough not to crumble in our time—to turn the eyes away from some sight which jars, and then feign a faith in its not being because we cannot see it—to dread nothing so much as certain things being found to be lies because our grandmothers who held them true ran safely in their grooves—to fence ourselves in with modest fictions, and then feel virtuously sure that all who declare them not to be facts are upsetting the order of things,—all these things have been done too long and too fervently for there to be social safety for the first generation that emancipates itself, far less for the solitary ones who see light through the darkness, and seek to stray to it through new paths.

Of course, when it is said that Charlie had arrived at the stage of doubting, it will immediately be understood that even so far she had not gone on her own unaided instinct. Women are essentially the undoubting section of humanity. Gifted as they are with marvellous powers of discernment, they rarely bring these powers to bear on anything more important than the paintings, powderings, and flirtations of their unmarried, or the peccadilloes of their married, rivals. When anything larger is set before them in a new light, it is invariably so set by a man. It has never been a woman who has first suspected corruption in either a creed or a cabinet. If they

have a doubt, they crush it. They like to believe in
a lot of things, the more the better. Calls on their
credulity in things of vital importance to humanity
are never made in vain. They like to have large
bundles of things that have been said and held to be
trustworthy for generations, put before them and
around them prominently, in order that they may
have something to lean upon. Whether they keep
all the commandments or not, they would willingly
see the number doubled, and this not out of careless
indifference, but out of a genuine regard for safe-
guards that have stood the wear and tear of time.
Whatever their practice, they are unfeignedly shocked
at the idea of defying any law which has lasted a
long time. Whether they crack the cords which
constrain them or not, they will avow that anyone
who says openly that those cords can be cracked, is
an atheist.

How very many fall far short of the requirements
of the human code of honour, who yet despise and
dread from the bottom of their souls any one who
dares to hint that some minor point in what is
declared to be the "divine law" is of the earth,
earthy. How many more who fear that if the
twaddle be winnowed from the truth, the whole will

be found chaff, which the first breeze that arises shall bear away into nothingness. How many who imagine that if a paltry bit of badly-designed ornamentation be removed from what they term, sonorously, one of the fundamental pillars of the edifice, that the whole thing will go to pieces and be shown a sham. Probably it is well that they are so numerous, after all. The "Brazen Head" was right, maybe, in chanting "Nought is worth a thought, and I'm a fool for thinking!"

The foregoing reflections, all loose, crude, and contradictory as they are, were the ones that filled young Mrs. Fellowes's mind, and considerably disturbed young Mrs. Fellowes's peace at this time. They came and went, they were dwelt upon and banished flickeringly and disjointedly, therefore to have thrown them into the form of a soliloquy would have been to have made them assume a position which they had not attained as yet. When women sit down and strive to think out and reason upon any subject for five or six pages, they do it on paper. At present Charlie had only arrived at the stage when one point at a time would come up and prick and rankle, and then be forgotten as another would rise. She felt that something was wrong

either with her fate; or with her will—perchance
with both; and she did not see how it was possible
to make the two agree.   She knew that there had
been a wild mistake somewhere, but whether Providence or the want of sublunary powder had been
to blame she could not decide.   She was sure of
nothing, in fact, save that she meant to do well.

One pretty, half tearful, half smiling April
morning she had been over to The Hurst, and was
hurrying back through the grounds, the nearest way
to Deneham, between one and two o'clock.   She had
promised her husband to be home by three, in order
to draw out a little plan or map from his rough
sketch of a proposed alteration on Lord Harrogate's
property.   Henry Fellowes thought he saw the way
to reclaim a large piece of marsh land from the
encroachment of the tide, and he was anxious to put
his plan before the owner of the soil as soon as
might be.

The way Charlie had chosen led her across the
fields that had been her husband's.   They were
Walter Goring's now, and were let to the same Mr.
Greyling who tenanted the home farm belonging to
Goring Place.   The partition-wall which had been
put up in ill-feeling, had been demolished as soon

as Henry Fellowes and Walter Goring knew one another—even before The Hurst land passed into the possession of the latter gentleman. So there was no obstruction now in the short cut to Deneham.

It was a very pretty day. There is a sort of girlish " when-the-brook-and-river-meet" beauty and simplicity about a young spring day that almost compensates for the want of that richness and intensity which are the portion of the maturer summer and more gorgeous autumn. All things look delicate and slender. The insects that make their way about amongst the tender pale-green blades of grass, are not full-bodied and bloated in the face as they are later in the year. Someway or other, too, the sun is more suggestive of all manner of purity and refinement than when his beams grow stronger and hotter. More suggestive! In the latter stage, indeed, they are not suggestive of purity and refinement at all. If one is not physically tired, the hot, fierce kisses of an August sun on the lip and brow make the blood leap. If one is tired, he always serves one as he did immortal " Mrs. Brown" on the occasion of her memorable journey to the " Victoria Theatre." It is useless thinking with the German sage, "I'll turn me round." When one feels the setting sun at all, it is always in the "small of the back," and forthwith a hopeless feeling of vulgarity and a wild desire to sneeze sets in. His brazen rays, in fact, make one feel wicked, or weak and dusty. But in the spring they are almost more silvery than golden, and they touch all things with such a tender light that the eyes that look upon them are softened in spite of themselves.

In the hedges and on the trees on every side, the birds that were come from the south were announcing their arrival to each other by their several call-notes. The blackbird and the swallow, the white-throat and the turtle-dove, were each singing a different strain with a widely different motive. But what wonderful harmony there was in the medley! Sincerely feeling the sweetness of it, Charlie tried to go further, and cheat herself into the belief that she thought it better far than any of "the operas that Verdi wrote." She wished to feel as unsophisticated and fresh as the weather and the scene.

On her left, a very little way out of her direct path, a little rivulet trickled merrily along, and its banks were fringed with the graceful alder, the weeping willow, and the tremulous aspen, in a way that was very fair to see—so fair, that she turned and walked up to it, and then stood, half hidden by the drooping boughs of the trees, whose young green leaves threw out the scarlet feather of her hat in strong relief.

There were little hollows or holes in the brook, and in them the water lost its crystal clearness, and seemed almost black. Tall bulrushes grew in sturdy clumps, making her think of the "Great God Pan," and the rare treatment he received in the verse of Mrs. Browning. Feathery plants on the banks were putting forth their young fragile leaves cautiously, to look at themselves in the water below. The bright black eyes of a nervous toad, who dreaded some disturbing influence from the young lady might injure her spawn, were fixed upon Charlie from a hole in the opposite bank. A cart-mare and her large-kneed daughter stood out—the one a chestnut touched to gold by the sun's rays, the other a bronzed black—on the emerald green of the meadow over the way. A fair harbinger of the coming summer, in the shape of a speckled wood-butterfly, waltzed about in the air to the music of its own thoughts, which perhaps were to

the effect that it "would never languish for wealth
or for power, or sigh to see slaves at its feet," as
Haynes Bayly avowed he would never do, could he
but compass his wishes and be a butterfly born in a
bower. All these things Charlie saw and felt, as
she stood there, to be as fair a picture of the boy-
hood of the year as she might ever hope to look
upon again. What was wanting? What caused
the weary sigh to float from between her lips, and
then made those lips close themselves in sad reso-
lution? What was wanting? "The touch of a
vanished hand, and the sound of a voice that was
still?"

The bright-minded gentleman who finds time to
write capital verses, amongst his other multifarious
avocations, has painted vividly somewhere, but in
what I cannot recall, the stinging pain of awakening
to the knowledge that the poetry of life is over. I
hope Mr. Edmund Yates will forgive me if I make
a mistake in them, for I quote the following lines
from memory :—

> "Yet I have known—ay, I have known,
> If e'er 'twere given to mortal here,
> The pleasure of the lowered tone,
> The whisper in the trellised ear,

The furtive touch of tiny feet,
The heart's wild effervescing beat,
The maddened pulse's play.
Those hearts are now all still and cold,
Those feet are 'neath the churchyard mould,
And I have had my day ! "

This is sad enough; but how about one who has never had the joys, and who yet feels that it is all over? The sharpest pangs of a memory that recalls bygone blisses cannot equal the dull, dark, hopeless pain that weighs upon the one who has nothing sweeter to look back upon than the knowledge that there would have been a possibility of highest happiness had not something else intervened. It is bitterly hard to feel that the poetry of life is over; but it is harder still to feel that all chance of such poetry ever lightening the road is past before one has ever read one line of it. On the whole, most people would rather " have their day," however it may be about the after-part. Memory must be a better companion than nothing. " 'Tis better to have loved and lost, than never to have loved at all."

She stood there a long time. Small wonder that she did so. The purling stream, the banks and trees robed in new verdure, and the smiling sun,

were pleasanter companions than awaited her in
that Deneham house. The hum of the recently-
born insects soothed her into temporary forgetfulness of the plan she had promised to draw out
fairly.

All at once another sound smote upon her ear,
drowning the babble of the brook and the hum of
the insects. The toad turned, and vanished, feeling
that it was no use keeping her maternal eye on the
invader any longer. The cart-mare whisked her
tail, and tried to prance, but fell short of her
worthy endeavour by reason of being out of practice. The sun shone out more brightly still as
Charlie looked up, and the picture was completed.
There, on the other side of the rivulet, rode Walter
Goring, smiling, and raising his hat from his head,
and his horse to the leap across the water, as he
caught sight of her. She reconciled the antago-
nistic beliefs at once.

She was predestined to meet him, and of her own
free will she went forward to the meeting gladly.

CHAPTER V.

THE sunlight glowed upon his broad clear brow, as he reined up at Charlie's side and bent down with his head still uncovered to speak to her, and she forgot that she had vowed to be very steady and cold and composed whenever she chanced to meet him. Her heart beat, and her eyes sparkled, and the colour deepened on her cheek as she put her hand out to greet him in a way that showed him all too plainly how glad she was that the greeting could be given.

Do we not all remember how prudent and exemplary was the conduct of "The Lady of Shalott" for any number of years? Vaguely she had listened to the tale of a curse being liable to fall upon her if she stayed her weaving. So she kept on steadily at her weary work—seeing the troops of damsels

glad, the plump abbots, the curly-haired shepherd
lads, the crimson-robed pages, occasionally even
gallant knights, "go riding by to Camelot," without
turning away from her mirror to glance after them
in the flesh. But when Lancelot rode along, she,
oblivious of the fact that queenly fetters fast
enchained that peerless cavalier, braved the curse,
and left the loom, and looked after the "bearded
meteor." Of course she was very foolish; we who
are not placed upon a little islet in a river, with a
loom and a mirror, and nothing more to interest
ourselves with, can estimate her temptation and
folly with admirable exactitude. "'Tis wiser being
sane than mad;" but a Lancelot flashing across
one's solitude is a fearful trial of sanity.

The man who broke in upon Charlie Fellowes's
day-dream was devoid of those gorgeous accessories
which strengthened Lancelot's charms in the golden
word-picture Tennyson has painted. He had no
shield with a red-cross knight for ever kneeling to
a lady in it—no gemmy bridle—no thickly-jewelled
saddle-leather—no helmet and helmet-feather to
burn "like one burning flame together." But
though he had none of these, he was all-sufficiently
bewildering. The young, good-looking gentleman

sitting his handsome, thoroughbred horse with the ease and grace of a centaur, or rather of an accomplished equestrian, I will say—preferring to draw similes from things I have seen—was as disturbing an influence to the modern-minded victim of solitude, as Lancelot in all his glory was to the type of, and warning to, her sex—the lady who looked indiscreetly, loved unwisely, and then had nothing for it but to die.

For no solitude could be more complete or more painful than was the heart and mind solitude of this wife, whose husband's eyes were too frequently glazed with wine for her ever to look in them and find companionship. To her sorrow she knew that she had never loved her husband; to her terror and remorse she feared that she did love this other man: to herself, however, she had vowed, that never, by look or word or sign, would she suffer that love to manifest itself. But when she saw him—saw him so near, when she had thought him so far off—when she heard his voice, and her heart's chords thrilled to it—when she met his eyes and the old truth struck her afresh, that question and answer passed between them without speech—when she marked that gladness sparkled over his brow and

lips and eyes at thus meeting with her, she forgot
all sorrow, terror, and remorse, and through every
fibre of her frame was conscious of nothing but
joy.

Why did she love him so well on so little? it
may be asked. I do not know. The spell was
wrought, but how, it is hard to say. She loved him
best in the world, because he was the best she
knew—the one than whom nothing ever could be
better, brighter, and kinder. She loved him
because on her darkest hours he had the power of
shedding light. In her hardest moods his smile
could soften her—in the midst of her unhappiness
the mere sight of him made her happy. It was no
mere blind, besotted, animal passion. He was
clever, refined, generous, and gallant; yet after all
it was not these things for which alone she would
" have left the loom." It was something else—
something which cannot be defined in words—some
subtle atmosphere which was partly the result of
those qualities blended with something else to
which she was sympathetic—a certain restrained
passion which, had he let it go, would (she knew)
have carried all before it, but which he never would
let go, or seem to restrain with difficulty. But the

best reason which can be given after all is, that she loved him because—she loved him.

Had she stood alone in the world in seeming as she did in fact—had no man trusted her with his name and honour, she loved Walter Goring well enough to have echoed Eloisa's declaration—

> "Not Cæsar's Empress would I deign to prove ;
> No, make me mistress to the man I love :
> If there be yet another name more free,
> More fond than mistress, make me that to thee."

But a man had given his name and honour into her keeping, and so she told herself in a fit of temporary self-delusion, as Walter Goring got off his horse and stood by her side—told herself against the evidence of her heart beating thickly in her throat, that she loved him as a brother.

" I didn't know you were home," she said, quickly, hoping that the explanation would satisfactorily account for a certain flushing of the cheeks, of which she was conscious. It was no bad tribute to him, that she felt that she would rather that any other person in the world than himself should fathom her feeling. Then she went on, " How is Daisy ? "

"Very well, when I saw her last. Which way
are you walking?"

"Oh! any way," she replied, forgetting all about
the "plan" she had promised to be home at three,
to draw out. "I have been over to see my sister."
Then they talked a little weather, and he told her
how he had been a couple of fields off when he
caught sight of her red feather through the
trees.

"Have you seen Frank?" she asked, almost
abruptly.

"No. I've not been in town at all. I went over
to Paris, with a man I know, meaning to stay a
week; instead of which I stayed many."

"So Frank told me. He told me also that the
picture will be wanted in May." Her lips trembled
a little as she spoke, but she covered the trembling
with a smile.

He laughed and coloured a little. "Does Daisy
ever write to you?" he asked.

"Never," she replied. She was longing for an
opportunity of saying something magnanimous, not
to say enthusiastic, about Daisy. It seemed to her
that she was a debtor to Daisy, in that she dared to
find solace in the smile of Daisy's future lord.

But she did not see a good opening for the magnanimity; if Walter Goring was a genuine lover, her warmest praises of the one he loved would fall flatly on his ears.

If he were a genuine lover! The thought that he was such to Daisy made her eyes shoot fire, and her heart dance, and herself hate herself for giving these signs of jealousy without right. "Daisy write to her!" No. Why should Daisy write to her? she wanted no letters from Daisy! She wanted nothing save—what? Well, nothing that she could ever have. It is horrible that such trivialities should so deepen and act upon all that makes life worth having—horrible, but true; but the smallest inflection of the tone in which he said the lightest word this day, deepened the love she had for him; and his silence was more dangerous still, because in it she had time to think.

"I hoped that she had written to you," he went on;. "those people she is living with are wide apart from her in reality; she isn't happy, Mrs. Fellowes, and she has no woman friend there. I hoped that she had found one in you."

It was not the tone of blind lover-like belief. It was the tone of a man who had a weighty sense of responsibility; he spoke affectionately, but as a brother might have spoken of a sister. Charlie could only reply—

"Oh! you must be mistaken!" It did seem to her so wildly incredible, that perfect happiness should not be the portion of the one in April who was going to marry Walter Goring in May.

He shook his head. His love for Daisy was no big overwhelming passion, such as he knew himself to be capable of feeling, did he dare; but it was warm, honest, and active, nevertheless. He had not come to the conclusion that she was not happy without pain; but before he left Brighton for Paris, Daisy had often been bored, and had frequently jerked her head away impatiently, not to say ill-temperedly, when he was kissing her. He had offered her her freedom once, and she had rejected his offer with a disquietude that led him to suppose that it was but the girlish doubt of how far it would "be proper" to go that made her repel him. But though he was willing to suppose this, he could not cheat himself into the belief that she was quite happy.

"I wish she could have stayed with you,' he went on; and then poor Charlie saw the opening

for the expression of that magnanimity which she
was longing to display towards the betrothed of the
man she loved. She forgot that her husband's
home was not entirely her own; she forgot the
hours of anguish it would assuredly cost her; she
forgot everything save that it seemed to be within
the scope of her ability to serve Walter Goring; or if
not to serve, at least to please him: and even if
she had "remembered," why she would have
counted years of pain to herself as nothing, to
the giving him one moment's pleasure. So she
said—

"I wonder if Daisy would come to me till you
marry her, Mr. Goring? Ask her—ask her, will
you?"

"Do you really mean it?" he asked, eagerly.

"Mean it? yes, thoroughly, honestly." She did
" mean it" thoroughly and honestly as she spoke.
She would have done anything to please him that
she could do and at the same time act fairly to the
man she had married. Had she been Charlie St.
John still, she would have counted her own happiest hereafter well lost in making Walter Goring
happy here, could his happiness not have been
effected at a lighter cost. As it was, she felt it well

worth while to risk paining herself for the sake of pleasuring him.

"You can't think how glad I shall be to see her with you, Mrs. Fellowes; there's something——." He stopped, and Charlie asked, quietly—

"What is it? Tell me."

"I don't know; *you* saw how it all came on with Daisy and me. I don't think I'm a conceited fellow, but I did think when I asked her to be my wife that her love for me was very strong. She did seem to care for me, didn't she?"

Charlie nodded assent. Daisy had "seemed to care for him." Charlie could assent to that proposition; but she knew very well that Daisy had not cared for him. Monstrously improbable as the idea appeared to her on the face of it, she could but fear that Daisy preferred someone to Walter Goring. But she remembered that Daisy had declared that if Mrs. Fellowes suffered a hint of the sort to escape, that it would be because she desired to see the engagement broken off; and the remembrance fettered her tongue. Of all things she could not have that said, and she knew that Daisy would be very prompt to say it, and "what would he think

of me then," she thought. Presently Mr. Goring
resumed—

"Now I sometimes hardly know what to think
about it. Heaven knows I would sacrifice anything
and release her if she wished. But she won't hear
of that, and yet she doesn't "—he was going to say
—"care to have me much with her;" but the
confession was a humiliating one, therefore he did
not make it.

"Perhaps she is so fond of you that she can't
help being shy," Charlie suggested. She knew
that she herself would have paid this man every
tribute of open worship, had she been permitted to
do so. She would have gloried in her love, and
seen no shame in making the most open proclama-
tion of it. But it might be that an equally sincere
affection would affect another woman differently,
and so cause her to act differently. She tried to
think the best of Daisy.

They had walked the length of the meadow
through which the little brook ran by this time,
and they had walked it very slowly. In order to
get out at the Deneham end they were obliged to
retrace their steps along the bank, and the water
looked so cool and limpid that it fascinated them

into standing still several times as it murmured a
running accompaniment to their conversation.
Presently, after once more asserting that he was
delighted that Daisy would be with Mrs. Fellowes
for a time, " your influence is good for everybody,"
he added, warmly, Walter Goring took a little,
thin, sage-green book out of his pocket.

"I have brought you something you'll like, I'm
sure, Mrs. Fellowes. Heine's poems."

"Ah! I don't read German," she replied, in a
provoked tone.

"But these are translations—the best I have
seen. Of course, they lose immensely in their
English dress; but you'll delight in them."

Then she took the book from him, and sat down
on the bank to look at it. After a minute or two
he placed himself at her feet, and asked her to let
him find the " pine-tree standing lonely " and thinking of the palm-tree ! And when she had read and
rejoiced in that most exquisitely suggestive and, at
the same time, simple poem, he found another and
another, and the afternoon wore on.

Under the circumstances, perhaps, Heine's poems,
with their subtle mixture of cynicism and passion,
were not the safest and most soothing things these

young people could have read. Their author's profound knowledge of the human heart so impregnates every one of them, that each says too much almost to the most careless reader. In their bitter gaiety, their mad passion, their abrupt change from either of these things to the darkest despair or the most callous indifference—they take such a hold on the one who reads them as cannot be shaken off. Alternately they plunge you into a fiery furnace and an ice-cave. The praises of love are hymned too hotly to be holy or "good for the constitution," as Heine says himself. The jeer at the inevitable failure of it comes too quickly on the wild rapture; one feels the whole time, that neither the madness nor the morbidity has a touch of affectation in it, and so are deprived of a safeguard against too free a sympathy which one has in reading Byron, or even Little's looser Lays. Paradoxical as it may appear, his very knowledge of the fleeting nature of all things makes him invest them with a terrible intensity that absorbs one. " We men who have no faith believe in so much more than you do," a world-renowned man said to me once. If I read his riddle aright, he meant that all things were equally false, and so commanded an equal amount of belief, which is the view Heine seems to take of the love he sings so thrillingly.

However, whether they were safe or soothing, or quite the reverse, Charlie Fellowes took to the perusal of them very kindly. The little streamlet babbled on, the afternoon wore itself away, Walter Goring's horse stood at ease on each leg in succession and found ease on neither, and still the pair under consideration sat on the green bank under the quivering aspens and graceful willows, reading and talking, and finding it all passing sweet. At last, fell recollection assailed Charlie, and she sprang to her feet, exclaiming—

"I promised my husband to be home by three! What shall I do? It must be hours after the time."

"Its nearly half-past five," Walter Goring said, looking at his watch. "Allow me to walk home with you and explain to him that literature and I are to blame for your forgetfulness."

But this proposal she strongly negatived, for she felt uncertain as to what case her husband might be in by the time she reached home. So they said good-bye and separated; and she walked away to Dencham with a miserable feeling oppressing her, that it had all been very pleasant and very wrong, and all her fault, and that Walter Goring would marry Daisy and be no happier, she feared, than she herself was.

CHAPTER VI.

A MOONLIGHT WALK.

No sooner was Charlie free from the influence of Walter Goring's presence, than she remembered all the things which she had forgotten while she was with him. She .recollected that she had intended being composed, not to say chilling, in her demeanour towards him; and she recollected the review. Then memory became a poignant nuisance as she thought of what construction he might possibly put upon her refusal to allow him to walk home with her. " He will think that I want to keep it from my husband, and throw an atmosphere of secrecy over it," she thought; "and I shall go down in his estimation. I can't tell him that I dared not bring him back with me, because Henry might make me feel ashamed of being his wife."

It was past six o'clock when she reached home; the dinner was on the table, but "Master was not in," she heard from the servant, and she was conscious of a slight feeling of relief as she listened to the statement; but the feeling of relief was of the most transient nature. The moment she came into the room, and seated herself at the table with old Mrs. Fellowes and Miss Dinah, she felt that the former regarded her as very culpable, and the latter as very thoughtless. "It's a pity your sister tries to wean you from your duty, Mrs. Henry," the old lady began, severely.

"Why, what has Ellen done?" Charlie asked, wonderingly.

"Oh, only induced you to break your promise to your husband: its nothing, of course. Mrs. Prescott supplies you with amusement and gaiety, and so I tell Henry he must expect to be neglected."

"Then it was very unfair of you to tell him anything of the sort, Mrs. Fellowes," Charlie replied, decidedly. She was very angry; the only thing that restrained her from disclaiming against the injustice that was dealt to her more determinably, was the unwillingness she had to drag Walter Goring's name into the discussion. She could not

repel the charge as to the evil effect of the fatal
fascinations of The Hurst, without stating where
and with whom she had been. She fully intended
to tell her husband, but she did shrink from saying
anything about it to his mother and sister. Petty
injustice from one of her own sex is even harder
for a woman to bear than petty injustice from a
man. "This is the first time Henry has had cause
of complaint against me. I am very sorry that I
forgot my promise to be home at three, but I *did*
forget it."

"Well, I should be ashamed to say it," Mrs.
Fellowes senior replied.

"I should be more ashamed to say I had not
forgotten it, when I had."

"I can't see that it's anything to boast of, Mrs.
Henry."

"I am not boasting of it," Charlie replied,
warmly. The reaction after the excitement of seeing
Walter Goring had set in, and Charlie was very
weary. "I am not boasting—I am only telling the
truth, and I am very sorry that it should be the
truth; but, believe me, it is not Ellen's fault that I
am late."

"Whose fault is it, then?"

"My own, entirely my own; no one asked me to stay, no one wished me to stay; I forgot it."

"Have you been for a drive with Mrs. Prescott?" Miss Dinah asked.

Charlie coloured a little as she replied, "No." She began to wish that she had explained at first to these merciless inquisitors that she had not been detained at The Hurst. Now there would be a certain awkwardness in making the announcement of where she had been.

"Did you stay there alone, then?" Miss Dinah went on. "I saw Mrs. Prescott's carriage go through the town, and I said to Henry, when he was waiting for you, that no doubt you had gone out with your sister."

"I think, as your sister went out and left you, that you might have come back to Henry, when you knew he wanted you," Mrs. Fellowes put in, severely.

Charlie began to feel as one who is baited, and her spirit rose. As they went on censuring her for nothing, the error of which she really had been guilty looked less and less in her eyes.

"I shall explain my shortcomings to my husband," she said, coldly.

"When he comes in," Mrs. Fellowes pursued,
remorselessly; "but he went out quite annoyed.
During all the years he lived with Dinah and me
alone I never knew him stay away needlessly at
dinner-time; such a thing never happened—never!
while he lived with Dinah and me alone."

"I wish he lived with Dinah and you alone now,"
Charlie replied; on which his mother plunged the
culprit into a state of penitential despondency by
shaking her head, and beginning to cry, and lament-
ing that she should have lived to see such a day;
and the dinner was brought to a conclusion in
thickest gloom.

"The path of duty may be the way to glory, but
it's a hard road to travel," Charlie thought, about
ten o'clock that night, as she put the finishing
stroke to the plan she had mapped out. For three
hours she had worked assiduously at it, and the
report which was to accompany it, and which she
had put into form from the rough notes which she
had found scattered over her writing-table. She
had worked at it assiduously, but she had felt no
interest in her labour. The embankment of Lord
Harrogate's marsh-land was a matter of no moment
whatever to her; whether the German Ocean or

the best engineering talent gained ultimate possession of the soil or not, she did not care. She performed her part of this task because it was her duty to perform it, that was all.

The fire had burnt itself out when she finished; for the last hour and a half she had worked unremittingly, being anxious to have her tale of bricks completed by the time her husband came home. Bright and sunny as the day had been, the evening was chilly; and now as she put the pen down, and pushed the paper away, the chill struck her and made her shiver. Of all external influences cold dulness is perhaps the most depressing. She was alone—she was in dread of the state in which her husband might come home after his prolonged absence in anger—she had been so happy a few short hours before. She was only a woman; so, thinking of these things, she drooped her head upon her hands, and made her moan over the mistake of her life.

The weary woman in the moated grange was agreeably situated in comparison with this one, the sharpest pangs of whose solitude consisted in the knowledge that it might be broken in upon at any moment. Mariana at any rate had herself to herself, while she was longing for the advent of him who came not. But Charlie Fellowes, however aweary she might be feeling, was constantly liable to a couple of litigious women, and a liege lord, who was too often in a state that would have made her prefer the society of some of the beasts that perish.

She had not succeeded in utterly concealing this change which had come over him from his mother and sister. Despite her best endeavours, they had seen it and sorrowed over it, and old Mrs. Fellowes had snarled at her about it. "Depend upon it," she had said, considerately, "if a man has never been addicted to that before marriage, its the wife's fault if he takes to it after." And Charlie had stood even *that*—the charge of having conduced to his gross excesses—patiently.

Meanwhile, Walter Goring was sitting alone too; but his solitude was so widely different from hers. His was so easy and refined—so well booked and well lighted, so fraught with everything that could contribute to the pleasure of both mind and body— so redolent of that charm which perfect taste and wealth combined does throw over the spot on which their forces have been united under good general-

ship. A charming solitude his; but one which,
nevertheless, he would have been very glad to have
had broken by Daisy or another. A charming
solitude, with the firelight falling flickering on the
pale walls, and deepening in the folds of the
pomegranate-coloured velvet hangings. A charming
solitude to sit and smoke a fragrant cigar in, wondering the while whether Daisy would ever play at
objecting to his doing so when she came to be its
presiding goddess. A solitude that was peopled by
so many objects that were dear to his taste—by a
Rembrandt, portrait of a monk, whose face was all
power, and whose forehead seemed to be tumbling
out of the picture—by a Velasquez, a proud-faced
woman in brown velvet, covered with tracery—by
one of Greuze's little French beauties, a sweet
embodiment of *sin*, the light of whose eyes would
have made many a man drunk—by a fine copy of
the Cenci herself, with that maddening mouth of
hers, and that fair fatal beauty of the brow—by a
pure-lipped "child" of Sir Joshua's, saying its
prayers—by one of Vandyke's cavaliers (taken from
his place in the corridor, because he was the
beauty-man of the Goring family), whose eyes
showed plainly that he had been "very bold to

take " whatever he wanted—by a marble copy of
the Clytie, with her passion-charged bust and
purity-charged mouth, with her down-cast brow,
and up-heaving bosom—by a fair erotic group—and
by a Leda, preparing to render up a passionate
kiss. A charming solitude, one in the midst of
which a woman infallibly takes up a better attitude,
and thinks more gracefully; and Walter Goring
knew this truth, and thought of what Charlie would
have been in it.

Perhaps even she, sitting alone in her own little
sordid ugly room, did not feel the full force of the
bitter bungle she had made of her life, as this man
felt it for her. By the light of her liking for him he
read her character plainly enough. He saw how she
turned to what was fair, and recoiled from what was
foul. He marked how exquisitely alive she was to
externals, and at the same time he recognised the
northern chill in her southern blood. Had she been
all a daughter of the sun, she would have thrown
everything but love overboard. As it was, there
was a dash of snow in her composition, which made
her graver perhaps, but decidedly less happy. He
had said of her once, that she would talk recklessly
but never act recklessly; and after the interview of

this afternoon, he saw no reason to change his opinion. Since he had known her at all, he warmly regretted that he had not known more of her before she suffered herself to drift into a marriage with another man. "In that case, Daisy and Goring Place would both have gone," he told himself; but at the same time he felt that "Daisy was a darling, and he should be very happy with her." Daisy was a darling! and as "Charlie," as he called her to himself now, was married, and neither polygamy nor polyandry were the law of the land, or according to his tastes, the best thing was to think of Daisy alone.

It would have been the best thing to do unquestionably. The worst of it was that he could not do it. The thought of the other one would intervene, and he could not delude himself into the belief about her, that it was "merely the old regard," a thing he was wont to tell himself about Mrs. Walsh. The thought of her as she seemed to him, a sweet, wasted, loving, clever woman, would intervene; and loyal as he was to Daisy, he could but regret that he could be so little to the other one, whom he felt could, under kinder stars, have been so much to him.

By-and-bye, as he could not shake off these

thoughts and the uncomfortable feeling they engendered, he got up and walked away through the hall out into the garden, picking up a Glengarry cap as he went. The sky was deep blue, unclouded, star-spangled, and above the silvery moon was sailing, touching a thousand points in the earth below, and bringing them into sweeter beauty. It was a shame to go to bed on such a night—no day could show him anything fairer. So he thought that he would go round by some plantations where the shadows were lying darkly, their boundary lines delicately tipped with silver. Round by these plantations, and past a pretty ivy-covered lodge, where a gamekeeper lived, and so home by another path. He determined not to take any of his dogs. He knew their propensities to go off hunting at wrong times, well-bred as they were; and he did not care to be obliged to distract himself from the scene, by having to whistle up depredating pointers and defiant setters.

As he walked along he could not help hoping that Daisy would come to care for these things as he did; or even if she could not care for them to the same extent, that she would invest a little more interest in them than she did in the fall of her drapery and the fit of her Balmoral boots. At present he could but feel that, on the rare occasions of their taking walks together, Daisy's sole thought had been how she could most expeditiously and becomingly get over the ground; and again, he wished that Daisy were a little more like Mrs. Fellowes; and then he fell to wondering why young Mrs. Fellowes had not suffered him to go home with her that day? He scouted the idea that would intrude, that it had been because her husband might feel a certain jealous annoyance. "It can't be that," he thought; "he surely can't bother her in that way." Yet what could it be? Charlie had been so much in earnest in her rejection of his escort.

The gamekeeper's cottage stood close to a gate that was very rarely used, which opened out from the Goring Place grounds into the Deneham road. Walter Goring thought that he would just go past it, and see the moonbeams amorously trembling on the ivy, and try whether he could not get over or through the gate, and out into the road along which he intended to walk to the principal entrance, which was some quarter of a mile higher up. As he neared the lodge, two figures loomed above the little garden hedge, and remembering that Dagorn, the game-keeper, had a very pretty daughter, he thought—

"Halloo! some rustic Juan sporting with Amaryllis in the shade; old Dagorn should keep a sharper look-out on his daughter;" and he began to whistle loudly, and to step more firmly, in order to give signal of his approach. As he did so, the figures separated; one went fluttering towards the ivy-covered porch, and the other came out and went hastily towards the gate, where a horse was standing, with his rein fastened through the bars. Involuntarily Walter Goring checked his steps, and sought to turn before he could be seen. In the man, who fled like a thief in the night at the approach of another man—in the midnight whisperer of dangerous words to pretty Alice Dagorn, Walter Goring had recognised the husband of the woman he admired and was interested in above every other in the world—save Daisy, of course. His heart beat thickly with indignation and several other feelings, as he saw Henry Fellowes mount and ride rapidly away. It was the worst thing he had learnt in connection with her yet; the worst, the most dangerous knowledge. "The dirty hound," he thought, "wasn't it enough that he should get drunk?" Then he thought of Charlie's frank fearless eyes, and of the honest defiant nature which was being taught and trained down by duty and necessity to live a lie. " If I were her brother, I'd take her from him," he thought, passionately. But even in that moment of passion he swore never to try to do it, since he was not her brother.

He walked on, though there was no more beauty in the moonbeams for him. His heart was oppressed with a weight of doubtful sorrow, that he could not throw off. He thought of Charlie as he had seen her some hours before, in the pure light of the spring-tide day, by that limpid water ; and as he thought of her thus, and of her sweet womanly warmth, his anger rose hotly against the man who had gone home to her from a flirtation with the gamekeeper's pretty daughter.

CHAPTER VII.

AN EMPTY SADDLE.

" Love in a hut, with water and a crust,
    Is—Love forgive us !—cinders, ashes, dust."

IF this be true—and who can doubt it?—what
is hate in a hut? or indifference, strongly dashed
with disgust and dread, in a square, incommodious
little modern house, in a mortally dull country town.
The cinders, ashes, and dust, which are the portion
of love in a hut, must be succulent and daintily
flavoured morsels compared with the mental and
moral diet on which the luckless one whose situation was sketched secondly must feed.

For about an hour after the completion of the
work which she ought, the miserable sinner, to have
been home at three to do, young Mrs. Fellowes sat
cowering over the table, with her face buried in her
hands, making her moan.   She was horribly un-

happy; her soul was very dark. The best she could do, were she true to herself, without a moment's wavering, would not brighten the dreary swamp of her life—it would only enable her to cross it safely. Was the safety worth the struggle? Was aught worth anything? She had striven to do right all her life, and this was the result. Could she have been more unhappy, more severely punished, if she had committed any number of sins, which might have been pleasant at the time? "It doesn't do to sit and think," she exclaimed, at the expiration of an hour. "It's only those who are well fenced in in pleasant places who may indulge in the luxury of turning things over in their minds." Then she got up and unbarred the heavy shutters, hurting her fingers with the iron bar as she did it, and thus distracting herself a little, and peered out into the street, trying to think that she was anxious for her husband's return. After flattening her nose against the glass for a few minutes, and seeing nothing but her own eyes, by reason of the moon being hidden by the chimney-pot of an opposite house, she went back to her writing-table and got out a chapter of the nearly completed novel—the one of which she was hopeful, the one that was to efface "Gerty Grey" from the memory of man. As she got into the swing of her story she forgot her dulness and despair, and felt that though her grand venture was a failure, that she might get up a sub-interest in life sufficiently strong to carry her through it cheerfully.

Her pen was not a grey goose-quill, but it was a clearly-running steel slave to her thoughts this night, and her thoughts ran quickly and brightly, as one's thoughts are wont to run at such an hour. For a few pages she progressed very promisingly. Her people had been rather stiff for a chapter or two, by reason of certain doubts which had assailed the mind of their creator, as to what it would be well to make them do next. Everything that occurred to her as desirable somebody else had used of late, and she had began to fear that she had exhausted her slender stock of original ideas. But to-night she had no doubt; the puppets fell into positions that were most awkward for themselves, and consequently most pleasing to the reader—of their own unaided will, as it seemed. The first sentence she penned was happy, both as regarded its reason and rythm, she thought; at any rate, it led her on, which is the most one asks of an opening sentence.

At last the puppets grew stiff again. The curtain drew up on a love scene, or what she wanted to make a love scene; but she dared not fall back upon her own personal experiences, and she found that without this she could not make them talk with a touch of truth, or move other than in a wooden way. Imagination could not supply the void that was made by a determined obliteration of the most she knew about it. Everyone who writes fiction must have experienced the difficulty at the shy stage of the outset of their respective careers.

The moment of hesitation relaxed her energies. She began to trace little profiles—idealised Walter Goring's on the blotting-paper—a dangerous propensity, which it is just as well to nip in the bud—and as she did it she thought how "well his love scenes were always done, and what a lot of practice he must have had to make them so perfect." She was but a tyro in the art as yet; she did not know that, given certain conditions, and the chances are very much in favour of everyone acting alike under similar circumstances: and so the life-like reality of the desperate love he made on paper made her fancy that Walter Goring had flattered and flirted with many besides those of whom she knew.

Then his poems again—those despairing wails, howls almost—by which she had known him first.

He was a very sweet singer, but, as is the case with the majority of young aspirants for the bays, the melancholiness of most things was much before him in his verse. She ran through the list of those whom he had reviled in old heroic measure, and forgiven with a broken heart in lines that ran trippingly off the reader's tongue. She recalled the ladies of high degree, who, in his first volume of "Poems of Life and Love," had always been doing dark and dismal things, in gorgeous array and high places, with composed countenances and corroding care at the core of their hearts. Occasionally even he had made hazy allusions to royalty—his boyish pride had been flattered, he averred, through two and a half verses, by some one who had in the last eight lines resumed her crown and sceptre. There was great consolation to Charlie in recalling and dwelling on these wild effusions of his earlier muse. She found herself feeling more than half convinced that the love he painted so vividly in prose was equally ideal.

Presently the clock of the town-hall boomed out the hour one, and a sudden qualm at the continued absence of her husband brought her back from the regions of romance to the real life around her. She put away her chapter with the barely begun love scene in it, and stole softly to the hall door, which she opened quietly. Then gazing anxiously up and down the street, she found herself saying, almost against her will, " Pray God he may come home safe ! "

The utterance of the prayer brought the possibility of some accident having happened to him home to her with hideous force. Supposing ;— but no, she would not suffer herself to suppose anything. She drove back thought, but she could neither quiet the vague dread nor stop the chattering of her teeth, as she stood there, looking up and down, in pitiable ignorance of the side from whence her husband or evil tidings might come upon her.

All at once the sound of a horse's hoofs, striking on the hard surface of the street, smote upon her ears. She listened more attentively, and recognised the sharp quick walk of the old brown hunter. Listening still, she heard the horse come on steadily till he came just abreast of a road that led away from Deneham to The Hurst, and then the sound decreased, and with a thrill of alarm she became conscious that he had taken the turning to his old home.

For one minute she stood irresolutely at the door, then she closed it gently behind her and ran off rapidly in the wake of the retreating horse. She knew the step of the old brown hunter so well. Those who are accustomed to horses learn to distinguish their steps as infallibly as they do those of their fellow-creatures. She knew the step so well, and she did so dread that it might bear its master to The Hurst and proclaim the open shame of the habits her husband had formed, to some groom or stable-boy, who might be roused by the sound of the hoofs and come out to know the cause of their being there. The fear gave her wings. She had fled through the street and into the solitary road that led away to The Hurst, before she remembered that there was anything out of the common in her doing it.

Her pace soon brought her close upon the track of the horse, and she was just thinking, "Henry will be furious with me I'm afraid," when, with a cry of horror, she came near enough to see that the saddle was empty. It was useless now to follow the horse; she let him go on where he listed, and turned back to seek despairingly for help and her husband.

All thought of keeping anything from anybody was over now. She gathered up her dress and ran back to the house faster even than she had run away from it. One frantic struggle with the door-handle ended in her failing to open it, and then she rang the bell furiously, rousing all the household from their dreams of peace.

Naturally, the first impulse of women when they are rung up in the night is to congregate together and ask each other if they "heard the bell." That fact ascertained beyond doubt, they light a candle, or rather strike matches, with hands that are un-steady through nervousness, and then essay to apply the light to the wick of the candle, under the aus-pices of eyes that are half blind with sleep. The result is rarely a success for the first five minutes, but eventually a blaze is achieved. Then they fall to wondering whether they had better go down to the door and tackle the invader there, or merely challenge him from an upstairs window.

This programme was religiously attended to by Mrs. and Miss Fellowes and the cook and house-maid, on the present occasion. Charlie nearly went

mad with impatience as she watched the flitting
about from room to room. At last a blind was
cautiously lifted and a window sash raised, and
Miss Dinah's voice asked—

" Who's that ?"

" It's I—Charlie," Charlie replied. " Do dress
and—— "

"How very improper of you to be out there at
this hour of the night, and—— "

" Henry's had an accident—thrown from his
horse along the road to Goring Place," Charlie
interrupted; " follow me as quickly as you can,
Dinah, and make the servants dress."

" Wait a minute," Dinah cried. Then she ran
down nimbly, and let her sister-in-law in. Now that
she was called upon to act, Charlie took her place
as the ruling spirit with a decision and promptitude
that almost paralysed Miss Dinah.

" We must keep it quiet if we can, but if he's
hurt," (at this poor Charlie's voice broke a little,)
" a doctor must be sent for at once—so bring Ann
with you, Dinah, and be quick." With that she
turned, and went off again on the hardest mission
that had been hers in life yet.

She did not run now. She knew that in any case

all her strength and all her composure would be
needed, and these she could not retain if she ran
herself out of breath. But she walked at a pace
that soon brought her well on the Goring Place
road, and then she began to look eagerly at every
place where the bank of the hedge on either side
curved and the shade was lying dark as a human
body might; to look eagerly, and to listen attentively—but for awhile she heard nothing save the
croaking of some frogs who were going a wooing,
and the chirp of the grasshoppers in the turf under
her feet.

Suddenly she heard a man's step—the next instant she faced the man himself, and with a cry that
burst from her heart, telling him all her loneliness
and all her helplessness, she recognised Walter
Goring. His first fear was that she had been out-
raged beyond her powers of endurance, and had left
her husband's home. It was almost a relief to him
when she stammered out—

"Have you seen my husband?—he has been
thrown from his horse."

"Not along this road, Mrs. Fellowes. I have
been sauntering up and down for the last hour."

"But it must be this road—beyond where you've

been walking, perhaps!" Then she told him
quickly of the evidence the horse had given, and he
could not tell her that he had seen her husband
start for home within the range of his (Walter's)
saunterings.

"He must have turned down some bye-lane into
the town," Walter suggested.

"No, no! the horse came straight along the high
road—I had listened to his step ever so long; do
let us look along here first."

He turned with her, and offered her his arm, for
she was shivering with the cold night air, and her
legs were tottering under her. Then they walked
along, looking and listening, and dreading that the
worst that could happen had happened to Henry
Fellowes; and Charlie girded fiercely against Dinah
for not following faster.

At last they gained the entrance into the Goring
Place grounds, where Dagorn's lodge stood, and
Walter Goring knew that the man they were
looking for had not ridden in the other direction.
"We may as well turn back now. I'll take you
home, and then find him by myself—do believe that
it will be all right, Mrs. Fellowes."

But she could not believe that it would be all

right. She was picturing the worst possibilities at one moment, and the next going through a thrilling scene of reconciliation with her husband, who might be just enough hurt to be grateful for her anxiety about him. The worst of it is, however fertile imagination may be in conjuring up miseries, one or two disagreeables of a very poignant order are sure to crop up when the end comes, and take us by surprise.

Very many years ago when I was a small child, and long before Free-trade was in the ascendant, I was startled out of my baby-dreams once in the dead of night by confusion and uproar and the words: "Papa is fighting the smugglers!" Now smugglers were a very familiar abstract idea to me. Papa was popularly supposed to be always looking out for them and "boarding them," together with the band of Coast-guard men under his command; but he did these things away from home, out in Blakeney Harbour, or the Pit. The charm of mystery was over smugglers to me. It was delightful intelligence to me that "Papa was fighting them in the watch-house yard."

Even at this distance of time I can recal the sensations with which I wriggled out of my crib, and

ambled away unnoticed in the confusion that
reigned to a western window that commanded the
scene of carnage which I hoped to witness. As I
ran along I heard an order given for "lots of hot
water." "That was for washing the wounds," I
thought. I pictured my papa surrounded by
smugglers, cutting and slashing, and killing them
with that sword of his which I liked so well, and
which I should have liked so much better if he
would but have assured me that he had ever "killed
a man with it;" but he never would assure me of
this. This blood-thirstiness of mine had been
engendered by desultory dips into " The Chronicles
of Froissart,"—a book which few children know, and
fewer still care about,—to the perusal of which I had
been driven, first by dulness and the want of something else to read, and afterwards by a certain
sanguinary taste, which developed as I grew in the
knowledge that honour and glory, and medals and
pensions, and "honourable mentions," were the
portions of those who had run the greatest risks,
and destroyed the greatest number of their foreign
fellow-creatures in the cause of that "Service" in
which the men of my family were steeped. At any
rate, whatever the cause, I had the taste, and on

this occasion I ambled off excitedly and delightedly to see my papa fighting the French smugglers.

It never occurred to me that he might be killed in the skirmish. I was too much accustomed to run my fingers along a deep sabre scar on his head, and to hear of sundry bullets which gave him great pain sometimes, and which were poured into him during a cutting-out expedition from the " Ganymede," off the coast of Spain in 1813. I was too much accustomed to hear casual mention made of these wounds for a single spasm of childish fear to assail my heart on account of my papa. So I ran briskly off to that western window, and looked through it, hoping to see his sword flashing and lots of blood flowing. Instead of these things, I saw a number of French sailors handcuffed and huddled together, while my father was deciding whether he should billet them in the stable or in his own house for the night. There was no fighting, no danger. The hot water was not wanted to wash the wounded, but to make coffee for the poor fellows, who were the tamest and merriest of smugglers—they were not even angry with their captors! I was bitterly disappointed. I pattered back moodily to my crib, and was presently found crying, and consolation was then offered me under the mistaken impression that I had been affectionately fearful that "my papa was in danger." At the time I was not honest enough to state the true cause of my grief, having the grace to be a little ashamed of it even then.

So Charlie Fellowes, wandering along miserably in the moonlight, leaning on Walter Goring's arm and looking for her husband, was conscious of feeling that she had not prepared herself "for the worst," when she came, as she presently did, upon Henry Fellowes.

CHAPTER VIII.

ONLY A WOMAN.

THEY had turned back, Charlie hanging on Mr. Goring's arm, and suggesting at intervals of about four moments the dreariest and most doleful of pro- babilities connected with the subject of the dis- appearance of her husband, and Walter Goring consoling her as best he could—as *only* he could; and wishing with fullest fervour that he could console her better.

In his own heart he had no very over-weaning sense of horror at the probability of Henry Fellowes having broken his neck. The man had let himself down so of late, and had this night put such a finishing stroke to his conduct, that Walter Goring, though no Sir Galahad, had conceived a con- temptuous aversion for Mr. Fellowes—an aversion that would have rendered it a matter of indifference

whether he lived or died had it not been for Mr.
Fellowes' wife. As it was, the thought of her
banished the indifference, and made him feel, even
as she trembled with emotion on his arm, that it
would be well for her if her worst anxiety were presently well-grounded. He felt so keenly the bitter-
ness of her fate; and at the same time he felt more
keenly still that any attempt on his part to sweeten
it temporarily would only embitter it still more in
the future. But, though he felt this, he could not
but be conscious of the subtle, unintentional flattery
of her reliant touch on his arm and comfort in his
presence—and, feeling this, it was hard for a man
not to respond.

They had retraced their steps nearly into Deneham High-street, when they heard footsteps and
loud voices advancing towards them, and presently,
before they could realize the possibility, though they
had recognised his voice, Henry Fellowes and his
sister met them, and Mr. Fellowes was as evidently
as sound of limb as he was in a furious passion.
Charlie took in both facts by the light of the
moon, and her heart began to harden. Her
anxiety about this man had been an agony for the
last hour, and now he met her with anger in his

face. What though he was her husband? She was
a human being—one, too, of a higher order of intelligence than himself. He could have been no more
than angry with a dog who had acted against his
wishes in ignorance and with good intentions.

"Henry, I have been terribly frightened about
you," she began at once, without moving her hand
from Mr. Goring's arm. "How did you lose your
horse and get home?"

"Alarmed have you been?" he replied, giving her
a full stare in the face, and a sneering laugh.
"Convenient alarm, madam; the next time you feel
it you'll be good enough to remain in your own
house instead of coming out to meet Mr. Goring."

"Henry!" his sister remonstrated, ranging herself up to Charlie's side as she spoke. By nature
Miss Dinah was a distrustful woman, but she could
not distrust the motives which had actuated her
brother's wife on this occasion. "Come home, my
dear," she went on to Charlie; "don't mind him
to-night."

But Charlie had recovered the breath which her
husband's speech had taken away, and she could
not take her sister-in-law's advice.

"Not mind him," she cried, passionately. "No,

—he has said the worst thing he can to me now,—I shall never mind anything else."

" You can hardly need my assurance of my meeting with Mrs. Fellowes being——" Walter Goring was beginning ; but he checked himself. He could not bring himself to offer an explanation to Henry Fellowes,—the doing so would be an insult to *her*.

" I don't need your assurance about anything," Mr. Fellowes replied, roughly. " I only know that it's a thing I'll not stand : here I come home worn out and exhausted, and I find my house in an uproar, and my wife roaming about the roads."

" It shall never happen again," Charlie said, coolly. " Good-night, Mr. Goring."

" I didn't mean anything offensive to you, Goring ; but I was very much annoyed — very much annoyed, indeed," Henry Fellowes said, holding out his hand to Walter Goring.

For Charlie's sake, Walter Goring took the hand thus extended, but its touch was loathsome to him —it was brought to bear so coarsely and so heavily on her. Then they parted —Walter Goring going back to his own place, and the Felloweses walking on to the house, where the wildest speculations were rife amongst the maids as to what would be the end of this.

The two maintained a strict silence until they were in the house and the door was barred. Then Miss Dinah spoke.

" Your horse is gone on to The Hurst, Henry."

" How do you know ? "

" Because your wife saw him go when she first went out frightened about you."

" Then why didn't she bring him back ?" he said, rudely, once more giving Charlie a hard determined stare. His mad unfounded jealousy had culminated this night ; he rejoiced in being able to show the woman who turned to Walter Goring because he was refined, gentle, and considerate, how entirely she was in his (Henry Fellowes') power. He rejoiced in mortifying the woman he had once loved so well—the woman he still loved after a fashion. He knew that he had lost all mastery over her heart and soul ; and so, like a brute, he determined on exercising the mastery that was still left to him. He would make her feel that she was his property —he would " break her in," he told himself. So he said now—" Then why didn't she bring him back ? "

And Charlie shivered to her soul as she listened.   He could speak of her in this way — as
he would speak of a groom or a stable-boy.   She
had grown so common in his eyes, that he not only
forgot that she was his wife, but appeared to forget
that she was a woman.   She shivered as she listened, and thought that under such treatment she
must surely deteriorate.   The best of her must be
bruised away by such coarse handling; and, as
she thought this, she hated him.   And she lifted
her head and looked her hate of his physical power
—but still held her peace.

Miss Dinah left them almost immediately; and
for the first time she betrayed that sort of feminine affection for Charlie which is shown in a kiss.
She was very sorry now for her brother's wife; she
pitied her profoundly; and she was terribly afraid
of Charlie being driven into open rebellion by his
manner, and so of a scandal coming upon the name
of Fellowes.   So she kissed Charlie's burning
brow; and, as she did so, she prayed Charlie to be
patient.

As soon as her sister-in-law left them, Henry
Fellowes altered his manner a little.   He had taken
enough wine not to be intoxicated, but not to be

one thing long; and his versatility was about as odious as anything that can be imagined. Having humbled her, as he hoped, before Walter Goring, —the man whom she preferred to himself,—and his sister, he now wanted to make friends, in order that the subject might be dropped till such time as he chose to resume it and humble her again. If any surprise be felt that a man so hearty, good-humoured, and good-natured as he was, when he first came into this story, should have developed into such a coarse, mean-spirited, half-tyrant, half profligate, let it be borne in mind that the heartiness was the result of full health and prosperity, that the good-humour came from good fortune, and the good-nature from an animal indifference to every form of annoyance that did not affect himself; and that none of these things were ever shown to be other than they were. When he lost the position he had been accustomed to fill, the pleasures which money enabled him to purchase, and the consideration which position and money alone command, he had nothing to fall back upon. His big handsome frame contained a very small mind and no soul worth mentioning. While it came easy to him, he had been generous; while there

had been no special call for it, he had shown a sort
of graciousness and manly consideration for his
wife that was partly the result of his thinking her
so pretty and graceful, and partly the result of that
deep-rooted dislike he had to discussing unpleasant
subjects till he was compelled to do so. In fact,
while he had been a prosperous animal he had
been a very amiable and agreeable one. But when
the prosperity vanished, nothing but the animal
was left.

The alteration in his manner as soon as his
sister left them, did not strike Charlie as being
either graceful or desirable. She had seated herself on her own low writing-chair, and he came
and leant over the back of it and kissed her,
saying—

"We have both been rather foolish to-night,
Charlie. Let us forgive and forget."

"I can't make the smallest pretence of doing
either; and I have done nothing for you to forgive,
or that I want you to forget," she replied, quietly.
She could not forget that Walter Goring had heard
her taunted with—she hardly knew what. She
could not forgive it. She had been lowered, she
told herself, in the eyes of the man with whom

she most desired to stand well. She could not forgive it.

" You must think that it was enough to annoy any fellow, Charlie," he went on ; and really, though he had brought the annoyance on himself, and fully deserved it, he was quite right as to its being " enough." It must have been altogether about as annoying a reception as could greet any gentleman on his return to his home, when his horse has previously arrived with its saddle empty.

" What was enough to 'annoy you—your horse throwing you ? or my being anxious about you ? They are the chief points of the case."

" My horse didn't throw me," he replied, irascibly. And as to your being 'anxious,' you might have been that without going out to meet Goring."

" What is it you think of me," she exclaimed, getting up : she could not bear his leaning over her. It nearly drove her wild to remember that he had the right to do it. " Say it out—what is it you think of me ? "

He followed her, and put an arm round her waist —drawing her up against himself. He was a little cowed by her manner. As he pressed her to his heart, a choking sigh burst from her lips ; but she remained passive. She would not cast herself free from his embraces; but how she abhorred them! Instinct told her truths.

" What do I think of you?—Don't take it so seriously, darling. I only think what's good of you."

" Then you told a falsehood just now, when you said I went out to meet Goring ; and *what* you have made him think of me."

Her words rang out so fiercely, that he started and let her go; and she sat down again, running the fingers of both hands through her short waving hair. The thought that Walter Goring would know now that her husband was jealous of her about him, nearly maddened her. This was the real sting. She did not know that Walter Goring had read the secret without any aid from Mr. Fellowes ; read it, and regretted it, and felt it to be too sweet a one for him to dwell upon with safety.

" You might have a little feeling for me in the matter, I think," he said, moodily.

" Feeling for you ;—ah ! it can't be all on one side. What feeling do you show for me? How you leave me ! How you come to me ! Do I ever ask where you go, or reproach you for what cuts me to the soul? No—stop," (as she saw him about to interrupt her,) " I don't want to make a merit of it—I know it's my duty to bear it all. But haven't I borne it? Have I failed in my duty?"

" Never," he answered, abjectly.

" And there's very small merit in that either," she continued, recklessly. " I have never been tempted to stray from it. If I had been—just ask yourself —are *you* going the way to make the path pleasant? I never professed any romantic love for you —God forgive me, I never had it to profess—and I don't tell falsehoods: but I *could* have felt so differently for you—if only you had let me."

The last words came out with a sob; she could but pity herself, knowing how her heart must have been wrung before she could thus bring herself to pain a fellow-creature by uttering such words.

" Charlie! is it too late? "

He was thoroughly sobered as he asked it. How he hated himself for having of late found bliss in revelry and forgetfulness in wine, and balm generally in flirtation with bar-maids. Still there was comfort in the thought that his wife didn't know the worst. If she would only forgive, and smile upon him again, he would amend the error of his ways. But a woman cannot forgive to seventy times seven unless she loves the sinner.

"Yes,—it is too late," she said, sadly. "The kindest thing you could do now would be to let me go away from you. Will you do it?"

"Never!" he replied, grasping her round the waist, and never heeding the sickened look that spread over her face. "If I can't have your love, I'll have you." Then he kissed her passionately, almost biting her in his frenzy; and her heart died within her as she took in the truth, that there was no escape.

The next morning, at breakfast, Henry Fellowes offered a full explanation of the cause of the old brown hunter and himself not coming home together. Need it be said that he lied freely. He had been to a distant market-town, he told them, to meet a man about "that embankment," not the engineer, "but another fellow" (here he grew sketchy), "who proposed something that promised well." Coming home at a slinging trot, the brown hunter had stumbled, and he had gone over its head. On recovering the fall—for he had been stunned—and getting up, he found the horse had walked on, and so he had come home a short cut across the fields. Even as he

offered the explanation, he could see that Charlie
was perfectly indifferent about it, and "by Jove," he
thought, "it *is* too late."

Then she offered her explanation. Not a word
had been said the night before about her having
broken her promise to be home by three, but now
she referred to it.

"You will find the plan drawn out, Henry," she
said. " I didn't get home till six, but it is all ready
for you."

" Thank you," he replied.

" The reason I was not home at three was, that
in coming through the fields I met Mr. Goring,
and he had a book for me; we stayed together
reading it, and I forgot my appointment till half-
past five."

She spoke quite coolly and collectedly, and Henry
Fellowes, though his brow flushed, felt that he had
made too much ado about nothing previously for
there to be safety in hinting at displeasure now. So
he only said, " Oh!" timidly, and then Charlie
proceeded.

" He told me that he is to be married in May, and
he wanted me to see Daisy before her marriage; so
I asked her to come here and stay with me till the

wedding. Now I shall write, and tell him that I can't receive her!"

"No, don't;" Henry Fellowes protested, faintly.

"Her coming would put us out dreadfully," Mrs. Fellowes, senior, said, crossly.

"Besides," Charlie went on, with a burst of her sex's irrationality, "Mr. Goring can't wish Daisy to see much of me, after hearing what an opinion you have of me, Henry; after that I should think he will feel that the less his wife sees of me the better; so I'll give the initiative by telling him that I can't have her."

So, despite her husband's entreaties, she wrote to Walter, and told him this, and he read her reason for doing it. He knew her so well, so very well, that he could but care for her warmly.

CHAPTER IX.

IT had been Mr. Goring's wish, from the date of his determination to marry his cousin, if she would marry him, that the wedding should take place at Deneham. It seemed only just and well that Daisy should go forth from Goring Place as a bride, as any other Miss Goring of that special branch of the family had gone forth. Therefore it had been an understood thing, and a thing that caused much commotion in the detached villa outside Brighton—that Mrs. and Miss Osborne should accompany the bride-elect to what had been her father's, and was her future husband's home, the day before the wedding; and the wedding was fixed for the 10th of May. Mrs. Fellowes' invitation to Daisy would have made, if accepted, but this difference in the original programme; namely, that the whole party

would have come sooner by about ten days or a fort-
night, and Daisy would have gone to the Fellowes',
while the Osbornes would have taken up their abode
at Goring Place. Now, however, since Charlie
backed out of her offer, the first plan was to stand
unaltered; and Daisy would be without that good
female influence which Walter Goring had hoped to
see Charlie exert over her, at that turning-point in
her career when a woman is popularly supposed to
be peculiarly open to impressions for good or ill.

There were to be no other guests at the marriage
ceremony and breakfast, save the people who have
appeared in this story—the Prescotts and the Fellowes', the Travers', and Frank St. John, who was
to come down with his picture on the night of the
9th, made up the list of those invited. Happily for
himself, some undefined feeling intervened and prevented Walter Goring from making a greater parade
than was possible about his projected plan.

Daisy had asserted that there was an absolute
necessity for her to break the journey from Brighton
to Goring Place, by staying in London for part of a
day and one night, in order that she might get
innumerable "things," which, at the last, she had
remembered were forgotten. Whatever was pointed

out forcibly, Mrs. Osborne was prone to see invariably. Accordingly, she now, as usual, took Miss Goring's view of the case, and agreed to go up to town on the 8th, and remain there the night, instead of passing right through on the 9th.

From the moment that Mrs. Osborne saw the beauty of, and acceded to, Daisy's proposition, Daisy was delightfully agreeable. She had been rather thoughtful, rather downcast, rather sullen, to tell the truth, of late ; but when this last harmless whim of hers was pronounced worthy to be acted upon, she recovered her vigour and animation marvellously, and forthwith proceeded to make herself delightfully agreeable to Mrs. Osborne and Alice. In fact, she overpowered the latter with presents of things that Walter had given her, and that were not strictly according to her taste. "He gave me this for my engagement ring," she said, handing Alice a little hoop of turquoise, " but the beastly things turn green if they get wet—you'll remember to take it off when you wash your hands, Alice. I always forget, so you may have it."

"But what will Mr. Goring think ?" Alice had suggested ; and then Daisy had shrugged her shoulders and replied, that "if Mr. Goring didn't like

it, he could—well! give her- another." Then she
stopped further protestation on Alice's part, by
steeping that humble-minded young person in a
vapour-bath of gratitude, by telling her that she
should "come and stay at Goring Place, by-and-bye,
as often as she could."

They reached London on the morning of the 8th
by an eleven o'clock train; and when they had put
down their trunks at the hotel to which Walter had
directed them, Daisy urged that they should start
on their shopping expedition at once, walking. She
was the guiding star, the ruling spirit of that walk;
and she betrayed an intimate acquaintance with
localities, and with the several specialities of different
shops, that caused Mrs. Osborne to look upon her
with awe, and follow her blindly.

It could not be that Daisy had any design in
tiring out her respectable duenna; yet it was a
terrible dance which she led her on that morning.
Up and down Regent Street, along Piccadilly to
Sloane Street; back again to some matchless silk-
mercers on Ludgate Hill, and always walking. More
than once, Mrs. Osborne faintly proposed a cab.
The May sun was a strong one that year, and the
pavement was hot, and Mrs. Osborne was a woman

of weight. But whenever she proposed a cab, Daisy looked alarmed, and said, "*not* a four-wheeled one, surely; all the people with small-pox and fever go to the hospitals in them, you know." It was useless for Mrs. Osborne to say, "those epidemics are not in town now, my dear." Daisy looked unconvinced, and gave pretty shudders, which Mrs. Osborne blindly accepted as being illustrative of fear, and entreated that they might "take a Hansom," which entreaty was not complied with by reason of there being a difficulty about all three of them getting into it. The end of it was, that when they returned to their hotel in St. James's Street, at half-past two, Mrs. Osborne was worn out by the combination of unaccustomed excitement and fatigue. The din had made her head ache, and there "was nothing for that," she said, "but to go and lie down quietly, and get to sleep."

Daisy waited until Mrs. Osborne had taken off her boots and her dress, and placed herself upon the bed. Daisy even waited until slumber had begun to press Mrs. Osborne's eyelids down heavily. Then she crept into her room, and spoke in a drowsy kind of tone, in order not too thoroughly to disturb and rouse her sleepy protectress. "There are some

K 2

things that I have forgotten even now," Daisy said,
standing in the solitary ray of light which Mrs.
Osborne had still suffered to have free access into
her room—standing in it, and looking such a pale-
faced, yellow-haired embodiment of truth and purity,
that a keener and more sceptical person than Mrs.
Osborne might have been deceived into believing
that all things about Daisy were as they seemed.
" There are some things that I have forgotten even
now—little presents for Mrs. Fellowes, who has been
so kind to me, you know. Walter will be quite vexed."
Daisy looked pensive, and Mrs. Osborne gave an
inward groan, and moved her tired feet wearily,
but resignedly, in a manner that indicated to the
acute Daisy that the owner of the feet was about to
flounder off the bed. Seeing this, the considerate
young lady went on abruptly—

" It would be cruel to drag you out again, Mrs.
Osborne : let Alice go with me."

" Mr. Goring won't like it," Mrs. Osborne faintly
protested ; but Daisy saw that her protectress was
amenable to the amendment.

" He won't mind it a bit when he knows the
motive—to get something that will show his friend,
Mrs. Fellowes, that I remembered her at the last.

Do let Alice go with me, and you rest yourself, Mrs. Osborne."

"But you won't be long now, will you, Miss Goring?" Mrs. Osborne said, suffering the charm of possible repose to come over her senses again. "I hardly like it. It's *not* what ought to be—you two girls running about by yourselves; but" (and she looked down upon them piteously) "my ancles are so swollen."

"We shall not be long, of course not. You'll see Alice back in less than an hour, and you know it's Alice you are most anxious about," Daisy replied, laughing. Then she gently went out of the room, and Mrs. Osborne blinked and winked, and tried to keep awake long enough to make up her mind that she ought not to let those two girls go out alone, and failed in doing so.

Daisy went back into the room where Alice was, and told her of the assent that had been given by Mrs. Osborne. "Your mother is too tired to come out, Alice, so you're to come as watch-dog, please; I am only going to a shop in Piccadilly. We'll go in a cab, and you can wait in it at the door if you like. I shall not be more than a minute getting what I want."

"I thought you were afraid to go in a cab this morning."

"So I was, this morning. I have got over my 'groundless alarm'—that was what your mother called it. I am not at all obstinate; I'm always ready to be convinced."

When they reached the door of the shop in Piccadilly, Daisy said again, "You needn't come in with me, Alice. Wait here, and I'll soon be out again;" and Alice obeyed her, partly out of delicacy and partly because she was tired. It occurred to Miss Osborne that the liberal bride-elect was going to get some offering of friendship for the lady with whom she had been living of late, as well as for Mrs. Fellowes, "and so, naturally, she would rather that I didn't see it till she gives it to mamma," Alice thought, looking affectionately after the peaceful, smiling Daisy, as she went into the shop.

Miss Goring paused at the first counter and asked for something. Before they could show it to her, she rose from the chair and said she would "just go on and look at those shawls," pointing to some which were hanging in the dim distance beyond an arch in another room. She would go and look at them and then come back for the embroidered hand-

kerchiefs she had first asked for. As she walked
along towards the shawls her heart thumped heavily. She was horribly afraid of one of the men
following her—one of the men who had seen her
leave the cab waiting and come in. But they did
not do so. They knew that the next department
was competent, and that their aid was not required
to bring the young lady and a shawl together.

When she passed under the arch she looked back.
There was no one looking, no one following.
One of the attendant spirits salaamed, and went
through the rest of the formula observed when a
customer enters; but Daisy passed on, saying
simply that she had been served. She passed on
and out at another door into another street, and
then she called a cab and got in, giving a direction
hastily and an order to drive fast.

She never thought once as she was jolted and
rattled through the streets, of the girl she had left
awaiting her. But she thought a good deal of one
who thought to make her his wife so soon. "Poor
Walter! it's only kindness to him though, if I succeed; and if I fail—oh! *if* I fail."

She could not even think of what would happen
then. A white horror crept all over her at the bare

possibility, and an awful sensation of sickness came into the palms of her hands and caused her jaws to quiver and open helplessly. A dampness broke out on her brow, and for a few moments she saw and heard nothing. In fact, she nearly fainted under the influence of the thought of failing in the something on which she was bent. But by the time she reached her destination, the sickly pallor had fled, her heart was bounding high, and her cheek was blushing brightly with hope.

Her destination was a house in a dull dreary street, in the west-central district, the door of which was opened to her by a shabby maid-servant, with a swollen face. In answer to her inquiry for some person, the servant said, " Yes, he's at home," adding, in a mutter that did not reach Daisy's ears, "It ain't often he dare stir out. Then she opened the door of a back drawing-room, and Daisy walked in, stood for a few moments trying to call to a man who sat writing at the extreme end of the room, failed in doing so coherently, and as he looked round and rose, rushed forward to him and threw her arms round the neck of Laurence Levinge.

His first words nearly crushed her to the ground.

"Daisy, Daisy, why have you come? Why won't you let us keep what little honour is left us."

She fell down on her knees before him, sobbing and kissing his hands passionately.

"You promised to marry me once. I shall die if you don't. I *can't* go on—I *can't* marry Walter. Oh, Laurence, let me stay with you! I love you so! I love you so!"

"You'll drive me mad, Daisy." Remorse for her, and regard for her, and regret for so many mad things, were tearing at the man's heart. He was not all a villain—no one is; but her love for him made him feel himself to be the greatest the sun ever shone upon. Presently he lifted her up and seated her on the chair from which he had risen, and still she clung to him as to the only thing that was dear to her on earth, and prayed him to let her stay with him, for she loved him so. To every argument he used, she only answered that "I love you so. I can't live away—I can't *die* away from you."

It was a maddening interview for him. In vain he painted his worse than poverty, his tremendous debts, his inability to go out even now in the light of day. In vain he told her that he was a gambler out of luck, and prayed her fervently not to try and induce 'him to add the sin of dragging her down with him to the many he had committed. He was paying a bitter penalty now for having tried in sport to make this girl love him. She was doing it in terrible earnest, and he loved her too.

Laurence Levinge had fallen upon very evil days indeed. It was his own fault truly that he had done so. He had gambled and cheated and been found out; he had swindled some of his best friends, and been cut by them. He had deceived a girl who believed him to be good and true, as he looked—who loved him so well that she would have given her life, her honour, her hopes of all happiness, to have served him, and who asked, who cared, for nothing in return save that she might stay with him, and this (it was his hardest punishment) he could not grant. For a few months, if her money lasted,—the few poor hundreds, which he knew he should risk at the tables, if he could touch them,—they might live. After that, she might starve, perchance; and, selfish as he was, he could not do it, ardently as she prayed him " not to fear for her, but to let her stay, for she loved him so." It was hard, it was pitiful, bad as he was, to crush her plea and beseech her to marry and be happy with Walter Goring, and finally to force her back into the cab, and turn away resolutely from her loving lips, and the eyes that were nearly blind with tears shed for this parting with him. He had been very false, very cruel. He had taken the hottest heart that ever throbbed in a woman's breast, and trifled with it. The end—the miserable end—justified her in thinking these things. Yet as he turned away, after telling the man to drive her back to her hotel, his wonderful beauty and the love in his sad-looking eyes made her swear that she would marry no other man, though she should not have the courage to tell Walter Goring so until the very last. "None but Laurence—my Laurence," she sobbed, fondly.

CHAPTER X.

"MY ELAINE."

THE 9th of May was the fairest day the year had seen yet. So fair, that one looked involuntarily for the hawthorn blossom on the hawthorn hedges, forgetting that what is customarily called "May" rarely blooms till June—so fair that women thought of muslins and men of cooled beverages, and every-body of economical plans, that would enable them to "get away" somewhere to be cooler in the autumn. Up in London, exquisite complete suits of the calibre of cobwebs dawned upon the vision in divers shop windows. Ubiquitous Gatti broke out all over town at once in feverish-looking ices and irre-pressible bottles of ginger-beer—a liquid which neither cheers nor inebriates, nor does anything, save painfully distend. And down at Deneham and all about Goring Place, people were saying that if it were only "equally fine to-morrow," it might be hailed as a remarkably auspicious omen about a remarkably hazardous match.

Daisy and the Osbornes arrived about five in the afternoon, and Walter Goring met them at the station, after the fashion of princes and other young men of mark when their brides-elect come dreadful distances to marry them. Not that Daisy had come a "dreadful distance;" but she avowed that she had done so when Walter remarked how pale and tired she looked. "Its enough to make any-one look pale and tired, Walter—the dreadful distance, and such a beast of a train," she said, looking away from him; and since no other was offered, he was obliged to be content with that explanation.

Daisy had made all things smooth and straight with the Osbornes. When she returned to them the day before, after that visit to Laurence Levinge, she found them, as she anticipated, rapidly driving each other mad by a series of broken-hearted, not to say idiotic, suggestions. Alice had waited in the cab at the shop-door as Daisy had ordered her to do, until her modesty and anxiety

combined to make her believe that she was the
cynosure of all eyes. Then she had made her way
into the gorgeous emporium which seemed to have
swallowed up Daisy; and when she did this, melancholy quickly claimed her for his own. In answer
to the most lucid description she could offer of
Daisy to the four men who simultaneously pushed
chairs out, and asked what they could do for her,
the sole answer she got was that " they would
inquire." Naturally, their inquiries ended in nothing. So finally, poor Alice went home in the cab
and a state of blank misery.

For about an hour, Mrs. Osborne and her daughter
made helpless remarks to each other. Alice's cir-
cumstantial evidence was flawless up to a certain
point. " She got out of the cab and walked into
the shop as quietly as possible," the girl said, for
the twentieth time, and for the twentieth time her
mother made reply, " Walked in quietly and didn't
seem flurried, you say, Alice ? "   " No," Alice
said, decidedly; but after this her evidence grew
weak, dealing principally with the thoughts that had
beset herself while she waited. At the end of an
hour, and just when they had plunged themselves
into an abyss of confusion, respecting what it would

be well to do—just as Mrs. Osborne had shaken
her head reproachfully at the ancles, whose inoppor-
tune swelling had been the indirect cause of the
mischief, and Alice had began to entertain dark
suspicions as to the suave shopmen having made
away with Daisy for the sake of the jewellery she
wore, and buried her lacerated corpse under the
counter—just at this juncture, Miss Goring came
back.

She did not absolutely assert it, but she implied
that she had been to her mother once more, for the
last time. She was gentle, sweet, subdued to a
degree, and Mrs. Osborne was too glad to have her
back safely to question her very closely. She
apologised to Alice for leaving her in such a way.
" But I couldn't have taken you with me, dear, and
so I had no choice, you see," she said. " I knew,
too, that when you got tired of waiting you would
come home."

" I was tired of waiting a long time before I
came back, Miss Goring," Alice said, reproachfully.

" Oh! were you ? " Daisy made answer, frankly.
" Well, that was your own fault, you know. I
should have come away the instant I felt bored."

"I hope you understand that it is my duty to conceal nothing from Mr. Goring," Mrs. Osborne said, faintly. She more than half expected that Daisy would reply that she "didn't understand anything of the sort," and insist on her (Mrs. Osborne) observing silence. To her surprise, however, Daisy only said, "I shall tell Mr. Goring everything, I promise you, to-morrow night : only don't you do it; leave it all to me."

She was thoroughly in earnest. She believed that she should tell Walter Goring "everything" —that she could not marry him included—the first minute she could speak to him alone. But when that minute came, her courage failed her. "I will wait till later in the evening," she thought, as her heart began to beat thickly in her throat at the bare idea of saying the hard words.

Young Mrs. Fellowes had promised to come up to see Daisy on this last evening before the wedding. She had promised to do so because Walter Goring had asked her, and because she might never again have an opportunity of pleasing him in even so small a thing. It was hard work to keep the promise at all—to come up and *see* him another woman's lover for the first time—very hard work ;

but as she kept it at all, she kept the promise bravely.

Daisy ("Can it be hypocrisy?" was Charlie's first thought) seemed strangely glad to see her—so glad, that Walter Goring could but contrast the greeting she gave Mrs. Fellowes with the greeting she had given himself. Both these women were so helpless—so apparently God and man forsaken—that though each felt the other to be her rival—though neither knew the full pitiful meed of help-lessness and misery of the other—they did, through some fine feminine instinct, incline towards and pity each other. Moreover, some subtle sense told Daisy that, let what would come, Mrs. Fellowes would be staunch to any professions she made in prosperity; and Daisy did not feel at all sure of what might come, even now, when all seemed made safe for the ring and altar to-morrow.

The poor little fair girl, with the dulcet voice and the yellow hair, and the eyes that but such a short time since had been so young and untroubled in their blue impertinence, was tossed about tumul-tuously by the very vague notions of right and wrong which had been sown by a shaky, vacillating, maternal hand in her mind. She was only sure of

one thing, poor child; and that one thing was that
she loved Laurence Levinge. Loved him in a way
that robbed the future of all terror to her. No hell
that he shared would be hell to her, she felt; no
heaven where he was not would be a heaven. If
through suffering, through sorrow, through sin, she
could have gained him—gained the ever-present
companionship of his beautiful fatal smile, of his
low, sweet words, of the atmosphere of the man who
was her god—she would have sought suffering,
sorrow and sin, and counted them all well endured
for his sake. But she could not—she could not.
She writhed under the fact, she groaned in her poor
misguided little soul; her heart sank away and
died within her, as she remembered the way in
which he had striven to make the inevitable truth
patent to her. Between them there was the gulf
made by those social laws which part us from the
living truth, and which men and women, with their
wits about them, are so prompt to recognise. Between them were these laws; and on her side
perjury and the position which a portion of her
nature craved. "If I dared tell Walter the truth,"
she thought within her quailing heart; "but "——
she dared not. She only bemoaned the truth, and

wondered whether she could live long under the
black shadow which it cast over her. Love was no
summer romance, no blithe pastime, no pretty toy
to her. It was the very essence of her being, and
Laurence Levinge had absorbed it all.

By the seven o'clock train Frank St. John arrived,
bringing with him the picture wherein he had
striven to immortalise Mrs. Walsh's beauty. His
sister and Mr. Goring both went out into the hall
to meet him when they heard him come in, and he
pointed to a large canvas-covered case, and told
them they were not to see the "Elaine" until he
had hung it to his own satisfaction, in a good light.
"Which room shall it be in, Goring?" he asked;
and Walter Goring suggested a little room that
opened out of the large drawing-room, which Mrs.
Walsh's taste had hung with pomegranate-coloured
velvet curtains. "The very thing," Frank said,
anxiously superintending the moving of that into
which he had thrown his whole heart and working
power. "When it's up I'll call you." Then he
went on into the room Walter Goring had indicated,
and the master of the house and Mrs. Fellowes
returned to Daisy.

She was at her best that night. The cobalt-blue

eyes seemed to have been brightened and deepened by the tears she had shed the day before,
and the cloud of yellow hair which fell in soft, full,
undulating waves, from off her face down over her
shoulders, had never looked more golden.   The
tears had done something else, too—made her face
of one unvarying pearly hue.   Still, charming as
was this increased softness and delicacy both of
colouring and expression, Walter Goring hoped to
see her look happier—more like a creature of flesh
and blood again, when she became his wife.

Charlie was nervously anxious for the moment to
come when her brother should call them to look at
his picture.   "I wish you had seen it before," she
said to Walter Goring.   " Supposing you shouldn't
like it?   I wish Frank ·hadn't sold it till it was
finished, and you had seen it."

"In any event I should have bid for it.   I was
determined to be the possessor of Frank's first
picture," Walter Goring replied.

" Supposing it should be a daub," Charlie urged.
"Not that I fear that; but I shall fancy whatever
you say about it that you were determined to say it
beforehand.   I *wish* you had seen it before.   If it
falls short of what we all hope, I shall go mad."

Charlie got up and moved restlessly about the
room, and Daisy presently joined her. "I care
much more about seeing your brother than I do
about seeing his picture. Walter has told me what
a charming fellow he is, often."

"I never used the adjective, Daisy; he's the best
fellow in the world. There, he's calling us," Walter
Goring said. Then he came between the two girls,
and as Charlie walked along before them he put his
arm round Daisy, saying, " Come and see my present, my pet."

Frank St. John stood with his back to them as
they walked through the drawing-room, which was
dark by comparison with the brilliantly-lighted little
cabinet in which the picture was hung, against a
pomegranate-coloured curtain.

For a few moments, as they still advanced, they
saw nothing save that the picture was a bright one.
It had been begun with a view to its being seen in
the Academy, and it was painted up to Academy
pitch. Moreover, it was an absolute condition of
the attempt at reproducing so bright a scene, that
there should be almost a dazzling brightness in the
picture. He had seized the moment when Guinevere, with full white arm still upraised, has flung

the diamonds down into the water, from whence
other diamonds are flashing to meet them.   Then
while to watch them—

> ———— " Sir Lancelot leant, in half disgust
> At love, life, all things, on the window-ledge,
> Close underneath his eyes, and right across
> Where these had fallen, slowly past the barge
> Whereon the lily maid of Astolat
> Lay smiling, like a star in blackest night."

Still with his arm about the golden-haired girl who
was to be his wife to-morrow, Walter Goring went
on to show her the picture, and introduce her to his
friend, the painter of it.   The rare likeness that had
been maintained to Mrs. Walsh, his absent goddess,
caught his eye first.   Then before he could look
further, Frank, looking very artistic in a black
velvet suit, turned round, and as he did so his eyes
fell on Daisy, who, shrinking, trembling, yet with
her gaze firmly fixed on the "Lancelot leaning in
half-disgust upon the window-ledge," and in whom
she recognised Laurence Levinge, heard Charlie
cry out:

"Why, it's Daisy!" at the same moment that
Frank St. John exclaimed :

"Good Heavens ! my Elaine ! "

CHAPTER XI.

HAD a brace of bishops united their forces in former days in hallowing the bond that had existed between Daisy's father and mother, Daisy herself could not have exhibited more unmistakable signs of race than she did on this occasion. The daughter of a hundred earls, whose mothers had all been countesses, could not have faced the position more gallantly than she did now. The gentle breeding which was hers by right of her sire, told her that no amount of weeping, wailing, and gnashing of teeth would remedy the evil and alter the past, while it would very materially complicate the mixed and unenviable feelings of her unwilling detectors. Therefore she neither wept, nor wailed, nor gnashed her teeth; she simply stood aloof from them all on the instant, seeking no support, praying for no partizanship, acting the part of one who could dare the consequences of all she had done to perfection, as Daisy always would act even at such a crisis. For the rest——

Frank St. John had met with one or two little checks in life, as may have been surmised. The navy had been his career, the one to which from his childhood he had looked forward, and it had been blasted, and an old schoolfellow, a boy, who had got the cadetship, from the Royal Naval School, the year before he himself had been so fortunate, had made things very unpleasant to him from the height of another " step," even before the blasting of that career. He had loved and unloved in a good many ports; had " been thrown over once when he had really been very far gone" for a brother officer. But each and all of the pangs he had suffered on these and other occasions, were light in comparison to that which assailed him now, when through him this slight, fair, innocent-eyed girl was brought to bay. Nice as was his own sense of honour—grieved as he would have been to see Walter Goring's perilled—it brought the first glow of shame that ever had been there to his cheek, to feel that his had been the hand to point out where the stain was. For he remembered the circumstances under which he had seen his pale-faced "Elaine" at the Opera—he remembered having described her to Walter as a "half-world"—and he knew with horrible certainty that the stain was there.

As for Charlie she was one of those people to whom a thing is never one whit the blacker for being found out. Doubtless this is an unsafe order of mind, nevertheless she had it; the crime was not in the detection to her. She had never believed that Daisy cared for Walter Goring; indeed Daisy had almost confessed as much to her, but had, at the same time, so appealed to her pride and honour, that she was fettered and powerless to protect him from the evil of the marriage. Now all danger of that evil was over—thus much was patent to them all at once. But she did not think worse of Daisy for it than she had thought before; nor did she intend to stand aloof from Daisy, as Daisy proudly gave her the option of doing. Her greatest regret in the business was, that her brother should have been instrumental in bringing the exposure about; for Walter Goring, she felt that there would be balm in Gilead still.

But though she was right in feeling this, Walter Goring had got a very bad blow. He had been left the guardian of this girl's honour, and now, before he had been in charge a year, he feared he was given terribly sure proof, in fact, that her honour was gone. He remembered vividly how Frank had spoken of his chance model and of her handsome cavalier, who would do for a Sir Lancelot. He remembered now how Daisy had been missing, lost, at the time of St. John's having lighted upon an "Elaine;" and remembering these things, and looking at Daisy, the living duplicate of the pictured lily-maid of Astolat, he could but feel her lost to him, and himself a defaulter in the matter of his loveless trust.

Have you never heard some high-toned vocalist fail by the portion of a note, and in the next instant triumphantly assert her claim to "touch-ing" something impossible more clearly than any of her contemporaries? Have you ever seen a spent thorough-bred drop, and pick itself up again before the eye has conveyed the fact of the fall to the brain of the majority? Have you ever marked the manner in which a man will buckle-to afresh when he has succumbed for awhile to the "examination fever," and the day of his destiny is near? There is courage in all these reactionary bursts; but there was more courage in the way in which Daisy held her fair little face aloft, and looked at them steadily from out of the cobalt blue eyes, when, after bending for one instant beneath the fact, she knew herself found out. It is useless to deny it. Those who howl and go down under punishment, no matter how well-merited, never command our sympathies to the same extent as one who stands the consequences, no matter of what, without flinching.

As Daisy stood it now. She was not cast externally in the heroic mould. No one would have taken her for a type of a gallant woman. She had not the lofty composed brow and the bony aquiline nose, with which, aided by illustrations in the annuals of a past era, we associate feminine composure and determination. Her nose never looked more resolutely turn-up than it did on this occasion; her forehead seemed to narrow itself between the line of her hair and her brows; her lips didn't close themselves steadfastly, or express scorn, or anything of the sort. They had paled for an instant, those lips, but they looked red and resolute

enough by the time anyone could look at them—
red and resolute, and ready to say anything. The
gentle blood told; she was brought to bay, but she
was quite ready to fight it out.

The silence that fell after those exclamations of
Frank's and Charlie's lasted only for a few moments; then Daisy broke it—broke it with her
silvery tones—tones that never faltered, though she
was so cruelly abased before another woman.

"Walter, you can't be too much disgusted with
me; but I should have told you"—for half a
second she paused, and bent her head the least bit:
the telling was bitterly hard; but she recovered
herself quickly, and went on—"what you see
there," pointing to the picture.

Walter Goring moved towards her; she had
plunged them all into a horrible position; but, her
eyes were so very blue, her wantonness, her wilful-
ness, were all so very babyish, he could but pity
and desire to protect her still. But she edged
away from his brotherly loving-kindness.

"No, Walter! I have been a deceitful little
wretch; but it's no use saying that here before
other people, is it?" Then she looked at Frank
St. John and fathomed some of the feelings that

were tugging at his heart. Suddenly she went up to him, and held out her hand: "I believe you would rather have cut off your hand than it should have painted my fault; don't think I don't know it, and so does Walter; but it is better, much better, that it has." Then she eyed Charlie distrustfully, and Charlie saw that she was so eyed, and did not quite know what to do. Perhaps she did the best thing that was to be done, in going up to Daisy, and saying as she did:

"I'll stay here with Frank while you go and tell your cousin everything you have to tell him, Daisy. I'll stay because you may want me;" and at that Daisy was a little melted. Female arrogance she was prepared to meet and repel, but not female affection.

So Daisy and her cousin—each felt that he could never be more than a cousin to her now—had a long interview, in which Daisy told him, as Charlie had advised her to do, "everything," with certain reservations. For instance, she would not tell him where Laurence Levinge was then, nor would she confess that Laurence Levinge had sought her to the full as much as she had him. According to her statement.it had all been her own fault, her own weakness. She offered to bear the whole brunt of the blame; she scorned the notion of any being bestowed upon Laurence. According to her, she had been the wooer and he the wooed, and Walter was fain to accept her version of her story through the dread he had of raking up worse things than had been already brought to light. That she had seen Laurence Levinge that time when she ran away from Brighton was evident, in a very ghastly way; but he would not seek to find out when or on what terms. The only thing of which he was quite certain indeed, in this first hour of darkness, was, that it behoved him to see her married to Levinge, and to enable Levinge to marry her.

Shall it be told how the truth crept through the house like a snake? A part of the truth—that is, that part of it which told to the eagerly listening many that there was to be no marriage to-morrow. Shall it be told how late into the night young Mrs. Fellowes stayed with Daisy, not questioning her, but just giving her that wonderful, subtle, reassuring, sense of womanly comradeship, without which we can't do, let us strive as we will? Shall it be told how Frank St. John and Walter Goring stayed up together, not because they cared for the endless

cigars they smoked, but because each felt such
generous sympathy for the other—such pity for the
fair, frail, little creature who was the cause of that
sympathy springing up, that there could be no
thought of sleep for either of them? Perhaps it
will be as well not to attempt to more fully portray
these things. They were done! And in common
with the rest of that night's work, they had better
be lightly sketched, and got away from as soon as
possible.

It was not pleasant to make the fact of the
wedding being deferred patent to the parson and
the parish the next day. Mr. Travers bore it like a
Christian; but, as his wife observed, *he* had not got
a new French white silk for the ceremony. "It's a
dispensation," she said, in the course of a call she
made on Mrs. Prescott on the afternoon of the day
that was to have seen Daisy married. "It's a dispensation, the sins of the fathers visited upon the
children, as we are told." Then, though she did
not word her thoughts, they ran on to the effect
that it was most inconsiderate of the ruling powers
to have timed the visitation just when she had got
a new French white silk towards a different con-
summation. Mrs. Travers was a very good woman,

with a great capacity for kissing the rod ; but—
her milliner's bill was limited.

Mrs. Prescott bore the disappointment much
better. She had not invested in a new dress for
the occasion, and the sins of Daisy's father had not
been the staple table-talk in her house for years.
Still she had a little pebble to fling,—and she flung
it like a——woman.

" Until I were quite sure of the cause of the
rupture, I should be very careful not to mix myself
up with the young person, if I were my sister
Charlie," Ellen said, with a little brighter blaze in
her cheeks than was ordinarily there. It was so
nice to call the girl who had so nearly taken a
higher place than herself in the Deneham neighbourhood, " a young person." There was nothing strong
or uncharitable in the designation—nothing harsh
or unfeminine. It was just a nice disparaging form
of notice that fitted the subject, Ellen thought; not
because she knew anything adverse to Daisy's
morals, but because she went on the broad principle
of its being well to think the very worst of her
fellow-women whenever their chariot wheels ran
roughly.

But Charlie was quite the reverse of prudent in

the matter. It seemed to her to be so very possible that there should have been extenuating circum-stances, though Daisy did not seem inclined to ex-plain them. Moreover, it seemed very possible to disapprove of a sin without striving to crush a sinner. Daisy still held to the course she had adopted at first, namely the course of giving Mrs. Fellowes the option of standing aloof from her alto-gether, if she (Charlie) chose to do so. But Charlie ignored the mute offer. "It's very hard for your brother, that his picture—such a beauty, too—should be what Walter will be ashamed to see hung in any room in the house! I'm very sorry for *that*," Daisy said, when Mrs. Fellowes was leaving her that night; and Charlie replied, " You see if Mr. Goring does not have that picture hung, and well hung too, and like it for containing the portraits of three friends, if only you'll let him, Daisy!" But Daisy shook her head at this, and seemed very dubious.

The following day—the day on which he was to have been married—Walter Goring went up to see his lawyer, having first induced Daisy to give him Laurence Levinge's address. Before nightfall that gentleman stood in the utterly unexpected and much " too good for him " (to plagiarise the title of a very

capital novel) position of being pledged to become
the husband of Daisy, on whom her cousin had
tightly tied up 2000*l.* a-year. This sum he had
settled on Daisy at a considerable sacrifice; but he
felt bound to make any that he could make without
being absolutely Quixotic about it. So he arranged
to sell such property as did not belong to the old
original Goring Place estate, including The Hurst
land. The fruits of this proceeding, together with
the large funded property left him by his uncle,
enabled him to secure to his uncle's hapless
daughter a sum that gave Laurence Levinge no
further excuse for not keeping the promise, the
non-fulfilment of which had nearly destroyed Daisy.
Nor did he want an excuse; her devotion, blind,
childishly passionate, dangerously passionate as it
was, had touched him. He accepted all the conditions which Mr. Clarke—who was far keener in
the matter than Walter would have been—imposed.
Perhaps the hardest one was, that he was to give up
what had been the sole thing that made life worth
having to him for many years—gambling in every
form, either on the turf or at the tables. This was
the hardest condition, but he agreed to it, partly
because he really loved Daisy, and had no desire to

impoverish her, and partly because one clause in the settlements set forth that, should he not accede to and keep this condition, half the money was to revert at Daisy's death to her cousin, Walter Goring, or his heirs.

"Did he offer any explanation of the heartlessness that made him compromise her so?" Walter asked, choosing the mildest expression he could find to fit Mr. Levinge's conduct.

"Not a word," Mr. Clarke replied. "He only said, when the business was settled, 'I hope Mr. Goring does not think me a greater blackguard than I am?' and I said, 'Certainly not.' He looked at me rather queerly when I said that; but he was not in a position to quarrel with any man's words. By the way, he said he should write to his mother and sister, and get them over at once."

"I shall write to Miss Levinge, too, or she won't believe him," Walter Goring said. "The sooner they come, and it's all over, the better. My poor little cousin! thank God, I was never harsh to her."

He was more thankful still for that he had never been harsh to her lightest caprice in a short time. Poor Daisy's dream of joy was a very short one.

CHAPTER XII.

WEARING AWAY.

UNTIL the arrival of Mrs. Levinge and Mary it had been ordained that Daisy and Laurence should not meet. Then Daisy was to go to his mother, and be married from under her protection and temporary roof. Until this arrangement could be carried out, she was to remain at Goring Place, where Mrs. Osborne and Alice still stayed with her.

The girl was rapturously happy now. So intoxicated by her happiness, in fact, that she never gave a thought to the murky paths by which she had come to it. For the first time since Walter had known her, he saw the little fair face with a brilliant spot of crimson on either cheek brightening the shining eyes till their gleaming would have been painful, had one not felt that it was only with

happiness they gleamed. "For weeks and weeks
she has not eaten enough to keep a bird in good
condition; so I fancy she's a little feverish now,"
Mrs. Osborne told him. Somehow or other, they
were all very gentle to Daisy; gentler than people
usually are to one who has done wrong, and dares
to be rapturously happy immediately after it.

On that night, when they had first looked upon
the semblance of Daisy shining like a star in
blackest night in the picture, Charlie and her
brother had been left alone, as has been said. No
sooner were they alone, than Frank began reviling
his task; the end did not justify the means at all to
him. "It's a foul start to have made, Charlie," he
said, decidedly, when Charlie strove to comfort him,
by declaring her belief that Daisy would have told
—would not have suffered the marriage to take
place, even if the picture had not saved her the
trouble. "I'm very glad that Goring has escaped;
but when I saw that little creature tremble, and
then get herself together for the worst, I felt like a
mean hound. It is no use my reminding myself that
I had worked in the dark. I feel like a mean
hound still. I shall never be able to touch a brush
again in that place in Sloane Street; the face of my

poor ' Elaine' would haunt me in every corner. I'll
be off somewhere — to South America or California."

"Oh, Frank!" Charlie gasped; she could not
help a little thrill of despondency passing over her.
She was terribly alone now; but with Frank in
South America or California, the sense of loneliness
would be deepened. So she felt for a few moments,
in the which she gasped out, " Oh, Frank!"

" Don't be afraid that ' I shall take some savage
woman to rear my dusky brood,'" he laughed.

" No, I'm not afraid of that; indeed, it would be
very good for you to travel, and I'm not afraid of
anything, Frank. Do go, and paint some Californian forest scenery."

"And get out of the way of thinking so much
about what isn't vital after all," he went on, meditatively. " Shake off the trammels of civilisation,
and try to banish the crushing notion that it's all
up with a girl who isn't chaperoned properly. Don't
look shocked, Charlie; I'll take up the notion
again when I return to England, home, and beauty.
But dropping it for awhile will be the only way
to enable me to spend my first ill-gotten gains
comfortably.

"And look here, Frank," she said, eagerly; "persuade Walter Goring to go with you."

He pulled his light moustache reflectively.

"Why?" he asked.

"Oh, only because he must want a diversion even more than you do," she replied, colouring slightly. "And we (the three of us) must give up that idea we had of working at something together; but you and he might write and illustrate an artist's tour through that glorious scenery with effect."

"Sage counsellor! I shall put it to him; the plan pleases me much," Frank replied. Then Mrs. Fellowes was called to Daisy, and the subject had dropped.

But it had been resumed at a later date between Frank and Walter Goring, and satisfactorily settled that, when Daisy was married, the two young men should start and travel, and work together for a year. They were to go somewhere, and do something; but where they were to go, and what they were to do precisely, was not definitely fixed.

Meanwhile there was little peace or pleasure beneath the Fellowes' roof. Charlie had once more repented herself of that burst of feeling in which she had asked her husband to suffer her to

leave him. She had repented and humbled herself,
claiming the fault to be hers, and entreating him to
believe that she had spoken in haste, and that it
was not too late for her to be the best helpmate a
man can have—a wife capable of being his friend.
But he had injured her, so naturally he could but
be distrustful of her. Earnestly as she laboured to
please him, untiring as she was in his service, he
felt jealous even of her having so small an interest
as her writing gave her independent of him. It
annoyed him, half unconsciously, that she could
get away in the spirit into realms whither he could
not follow her. And when her second novel came
out, as it did about this time, and she was paid a
price that made a very important addition to the
family exchequer for it, he took up the narrow-
minded notion that she was always remembering
the fact, and wanting to spend the money on
herself.

Moreover, there were other stings in that novel
for him. He tried to trace the characters back into
real life, and to find out whether they had any of
them ever stood in similar relations to her that they
did to one another; whether they had ever whispered the soft nothings into her ear, or listened to

the sweet words from her lips, which were scattered
so freely over her pages. He did not understand
that she simply painted, as well as she could, things
which she had seen, heard, and read about, super-
ficially, probably enough, but still up to a certain
point clear-sightedly. He did not understand that
she painted these things backwards, as it were,
arguing from effect to cause, instead of following
the commoner (and better) practice of analogism.
Some of the experiences had such a genuine ring
about them, that, forgetting the happy feminine
faculty of arriving at a probability through an in-
ductive process which can hardly be explained—
forgetting this, Mr. Fellowes chose to believe that
the experiences were autobiographical, and so grew
more jealous than ever. Consequently there was
little peace or pleasure beneath the Fellowes' roof,
but Charlie made no' sign by which an outsider
should guess so much. She was striving honestly
to teach herself to " suffer and be strong," and the
lesson, hard as it was, was nearly learnt now.

As the day approached for the Levinges to arrive
and claim her, Daisy grew nearly wild with impatience. She had ceased to observe any sort of
reticence now with regard to Laurence to Mrs. Fel-

lowes. The love which had been gnawing at and fretting her like a prisoned bird for so long a time was let loose now, and it revelled in the liberty. She would talk of him, of his beauty, his tenderness, of the tone of his voice, and the light of the eyes that had gone into her soul, till she panted with agitation, and the loving words would not fall coherently from her lips. She counted the hours—the minutes almost—that were bringing her nearer to him by their flight. And then, when she would cease from sheer exhaustion, and they would pray her to be calmer, she would quote Cleopatra's request for Mandrogora, "the only bit of Shakespeare for which she cared," she said, and pity them for never having known what she felt in the love of Laurence Levinge. "What do you think Mrs. Osborne says to me?" she asked Charlie; "'that when she was going to be married to Mr. Osborne she should have blushed to talk about it so much as I do.' Who cares what she'd have done? I daresay I should have blushed too if I had been going to marry old Osborne, in his table-cloth cravat and broad-brimmed hat; as if *she* could know anything at all about it with an old Osborne. I can neither eat nor sleep for joy, and I'll tell the truth about it."

This was said two days before the one on which she was to go up to town, and Charlie looked at her with a vague sense of pity, despite that brilliantly pourtrayed happiness. The not eating or sleeping of which Daisy spoke so lightly was beginning to alarm them all. She looked too transparent when she was flushed crimson in the face; the rounded lines of her figure were gone.

That night she sat and sang to them in the little room her father had had furnished for her. Good and self-forgetting as Walter was, he had some feeling which prevented him liking to be with her in the beautiful little room which he had had fitted up as a boudoir for her, when he thought she was to be his bride. So they sat this night in the old place where she had so often sang to them when the Walshes were staying at Goring Place.

There were only two or three candles burning, and the room was lofty, consequently the light was dim. For a time she sang brilliant opera airs alone, but at last she stopped, saying she would sing something " sweet and tender, like the light;" and then she sang more sweetly than he had ever heard her sing before—with more pathos, more feeling—"I'm wearing away to the land of the leal."

They all—Walter, Mrs. Osborne, Frank St. John, and Alice—drew nearer to her as she sang, and they were all most strangely thrilled. She did not seem to heed them, but sang it through—nearly through. She was striking the last chord, her glorious voice was floating away on the last note, filling the air with a strain than which no sweeter can be heard in heaven, when her head went down, the song changed to a cry, and a stream of blood chased the music through her lips. At the height of her fullest happiness she had sung her own death-strain. They knew at once that she had broken a blood-vessel, and they knew all too soon that she was "wearing away to the land of the leal" with fearful speed.

She died before her lover, summoned though he was at once, could reach her—before she had time to feel much regret at the thoughts of dying at all. Up to almost the last she could not realise it, urging that "she was too young and too happy to die." But suddenly the truth came home to her, and then her sole thought was of Laurence.

"Poor Laurence! Let him have all the money, Walter. You're so good you will, I know; and be his friend, because I've died for love of him, you know. Be his friend, will you?"

So she wore away, pleading for the man "for love" of whom she had died.

CHAPTER XIII.

Poor Daisy's last words, "You'll let Laurence have the money, and you'll be his friend because I loved him so," were strongly in Mr. Goring's mind when he met Laurence Levinge immediately on the latter's entrance into the house. There was no need to tell Levinge that Daisy was dead—he had heard that already. There was no need to reproach him for aught concerning her; clearly he was reproaching himself bitterly enough. Moreover, no one else felt inclined to do anything, save to try and comfort the man who had been so richly loved by Daisy.

He went alone into the room where she was lying, with the life still upon her yellow hair, but death within her eyes—into the room where there was solemn quiet, and a sad soft light; and, stranger than all, a Daisy who was for the first time cold even to him. Mrs. Osborne had prepared some platitudes wherewith to console the bereaved man. She was ready to tell him that he " must hope to meet Miss Goring above," after the manner of material-minded people, who will persist in offering spiritual comfort to others in defiance of their own practice. As Laurence Levinge bent over the waxen cold form of the girl who had loved him so hotly, he was too far from feeling that love is the soul's alone, for Mrs. Osborne's contemplated consolations to stand any chance of having a soothing effect upon him.

He stayed in the room a long time, not mouthing out a long-winded monologue on the vanity of human hopes — scarcely thinking, indeed ; only feeling, that Daisy was dead. He was too completely stunned by this even to muse upon the matchless organisation of the divine system of rewards and punishments. It was to occur to him afterwards, that Daisy, who had been more sinned against than sinning from the hour of her birth, was cut off in the flower of her youth at the very moment that the cup of joy was about to be offered to her, while he—lived ; and, by her will, was well endowed with the goods of this world. These things were to occur to him afterwards, but as he stood looking at her he only felt that the sweet child who was to have been his bride was dead, and that he was the cause of her death.

His face was as white as the corpse when he came at last out of the room. His impulse was to get away out of the house unseen; words of any sort from any one would be too much for him, he felt. But he checked the impulse for her dear sake, and so Mrs. Osborne had an opportunity of offering her crumbs of comfort.

It had been Walter Goring's intention to put the picture, wherein the story was all too plainly told, away out of sight while Laurence Levinge was there. " It's no use cutting the poor fellow to pieces with remorse ; my darling Daisy would re-buke me from her grave if I did it," he had said to Mrs. Fellowes ; but she took a different view of the matter.

" He knows about it—she wrote and told him, I know. Don't seem to hide it from him. It will be kinder to let it hang than if you let him suppose you shrink from his seeing it."

So, on Charlie's advice, the " Lily of Astolat,"

Daisy's parallel, was still hanging when Laurence Levinge came down, and he soon found it out; and, rather to the surprise of those who knew where, and when, and how Frank had seen his poor "Elaine," commenced talking about it.

"My poor little darling," he said, mournfully, to Walter Goring, "I was trying to be generous to her that night I took her to the Opera, little knowing I was breaking her heart. From the time she had rushed up to me—half frantic, because she had seen her mother, and her mother's husband wouldn't let them speak to each other—from that time, till she left and came down here, she was under the protection of my landlady, a good woman, who thought she was my sister. That night I was trying to make her understand the truth—that it was for her well-being that I wouldn't marry her, and drag her down with me."

"Levinge," Walter Goring began, earnestly—then he checked himself—"no, no, I'll ask you nothing," he added.

"You may ask what you will," the other replied, eagerly; "but before you ask anything, I'll tell you that heartless as my false prudence and cowardly fear of poverty with a wife made me, I have not the sin on my soul of having wronged *her*. I loved her too well," he added, hastily. "She was as pure as her prototype," and he pointed to the picture as he spoke.

Directly after Daisy's funeral, Laurence Levinge went away. A great restlessness was upon him; he could find no rest for the sole of his foot, as it seemed. He met his mother and sister. Ah! how futile their journey was proved: and there was something in his face that made them spare all semblance of reproach; though they had come charged with it. "Come back with us and lead a new life, Laurence," his sister said to him. "You will never forget her—at least, you never ought to forget the poor loving child—but you'll think about her less miserably if you're with us. Come back to Rome."

But he refused, averring that he could not settle down just yet. He would "wander about for a few months—or a year, and then rejoin them," he promised. Then he left England, and as he will appear no more in these pages, it may as well be stated that he never kept that promise. He "wandered about" for a time, trying to train down memory by day, by walking long distances in all

sorts of weather; and at night he could not bear
to sleep for the dread he had of dreaming. It was
for love of him that Daisy died; but Daisy's friends
had no feeling but one of sorrow when, in little
more than a year after she had sung her own death-
strain, they heard from Mary Levinge, who had heard
it from a hotel-keeper, that her brother had fallen
a victim to a low fever which had come on after a
long-sustained and successful struggle to save an
unfortunate woman from drowning in the Sorge,
near Vaucluse. So for the best action of his life,
he was rewarded by being taken from the world of
which he was so weary. At his death the money
which Daisy had implored that he might be suffered
to have, came back to Mr. Goring; and so, at last, all
things were precisely as if his uncle's daughter—his
dearly loved, wilful ward—had never existed.

Meanwhile Frank St. John and Walter Goring
were redeeming their time manfully. They took an
"artist's tour," that was really worthy of the name,
writing and illustrating it as they went. The scene
of their operations were the plains, forests, and
mining districts of California, and they took up the
life of hunters, living in a log hut, riding unbroken
little Mexican mustangs, depending on their guns

for everything they ate, " save flour and sardines."
Frank wrote to Charlie. So they stayed about in
the Californian solitudes for a year and a half,
during which time Goring Place was delivered over
to a housekeeper, and swathed in brown holland.
At the expiration of that time Frank was obliged
to quit his companion and come home for two
reasons, one of which shall be given at greater
length in another chapter. The other, and second-
ary reason, may be stated briefly: their mutual work,
" The Artist's Tour," was ready, and Frank was to
come home and see it through the press. The
literary part of it was entirely Goring's work; and
at first it had been decided that he should be the
one to come home and see it brought out. But
circumstances occurred to alter this decision. He
felt that he was better away from England for a
time, and Frank felt that he was most sorely needed
there. So they parted, and Charlie, who knew
that they were to do so, and which of them was
to remain, had direful dreams of Walter Goring
being devoured by bears and other monsters of the
wilds.

The chief cheerers of his solitude even while
Frank was with him—the only extraneous cheering

influence that came to him after Frank left—were
the long letters that he received, at long invervals,
from his old friend, Mrs. Walsh. She knew nothing
of the discovery of Daisy's perfidy to him, and the
consequent disannulling of his marriage with Daisy.
She only knew that Daisy had died, and so she
wrote to him as a sister might do to a widowed
brother, and said more generous things of the
buried Daisy than she had ever brought her tongue
to utter of the living one.

Mrs. Walsh had lived abroad for some months;
at first in quaint old Nuremberg, and afterwards in
brilliant Vienna, and both places had been equally
barren to her. She was not a woman to adapt herself easily to a new life—she was essentially one
who required to be sought, and who never could
bring herself to seek; and as it was the character-
istic of her beauty to look colder and prouder than
she was, few cared or dared to seek her. Consequently, the quiet dull city and the gay capital
were equally barren to her—in both she was alone.
Not all the memories she could scrape together, in
the one of the cobbler-bard and Albrecht Dürer—
not all the beauty of those blue Franconian moun-
tains which loom above the town, or the " fountains

wrought with richest splendour standing in the common mart"—could keep her mind away from dwelling constantly on the past. Of old, she had heard Walter Goring and her husband talk of these things—of the grand mediæval aspect of the place; of the venerable old iron-bound linden planted in the court-yard of the castle by Cunigunde; and hearing them speak of these things, and of the Old World atmosphere in which they were steeped, she had desired to see them. Now, she was seeing them daily—living in their midst—and it was all emptiness. So at last she gave up the cultivation of the mediæval mind in Nuremberg, and went to Vienna, and found it all emptiness there, too. Finally, she obeyed her instinct, and went back to her cottage in Deneham about the same time that Frank St. John, away in the wilds of California, felt that there was a strong reason for his return to England. "I will go back, and stay in that cottage until Walter comes home, in order that I may see him, and assure myself that it is all over," she thought. "I believe it to be—he is a dear brother to me now; but I will see him, and test myself, and at the end of my three years' lease I'll leave the place, and try my old London life again." "Try my old London life again!" Rather a hopeless phrase for a completely-cured woman.

Her old London life! As if she could ever taste the flavour of it again! She could have the old society very probably, the old style of dinners and drives, of "drums" and operas, the old round of shopping and calling, and general fatigue in the social mart. All these she could have; but that would be missing which had given them all the requisite zest. No; the old life would soon be proved a mistake, she knew it. What she needed was a new life—a new interest. "I'm only thirty-three," she said to herself on the morning after her return to her Deneham cottage, while looking at the reflection of her face in the glass. "Time has flown by on the wings of a dove for me, but he has not marked his flight by the feet of the crow yet. In the course of nature, my life is not half spent even yet; the best of it *shall not* be barren because Walter Goring is——"

What? She did not know how to phrase it. "Blind" had been on the tip of her tongue; but was he blind, after all? Did he not see her fairest of the fair, and feel indifferent to the fact? Then she recalled the expression of his eyes when he had

lifted them to her face after bending over her hand
and kissing it, and calling her his goddess! What
a pity it is that a woman cannot forget the tender
thrill of lips that have thrilled many another hand
maybe. The loving deference of the action may
mean so little; but it is stamped indelibly on the
recipient's memory. It may mean nothing; but to
a woman it always means so much!

She was haunted by him as he had been, and
" that was why," so she told herself, " she so longed
to see him again as he was." If he only came, and
was friendly—not frigidly friendly, but friendly after
the manner of a man who likes you very much, and
knows you like him, and yet feels and shows that
he feels that you can get on very well without him
—if he would only come and be this, it would all
be well. " I've idealised him in his absence, because
I have been dull," she told herself; " if he comes
and shows me that he likes me very much, and
thinks me an excellent woman, and—nothing more,
my folly will kill itself."

All these contradictory soliloquies betokened a
very wavering frame of mind. Of course they did;
they betrayed the truth. She loved the man;
naturally she veered about perpetually, and said

many things that would not agree with the rest
about him. But during every phase she wrote to
him as a sister might have done, feeling that her
love was half the offspring of habit, and that circumstances might arise again which would render it
expedient for her to crush it. " My folly will kill
itself if——" he adopts precisely the line of conduct
best calculated to conduce to the suicide. That
was what she said, or rather that was what she
meant. The danger was, that he might come and
make the expediency of her folly killing itself patent
to her in some other way than that which has been
sketched above. How, if he married some one
else ? Oh ! it was far better, she thought, to put
herself where she should " see him at once when he
came home again—see him, and show him that he
was free to do even that." Then she took herself
to task for the wording of that phrase even. " Free
to do that !" Was he not " free ? " Had he not
always been, and shown that he knew that he was
free ? But it is so very hard to think by line and
rule when the heart is much in the subject thought
about.

The romance was over, and it would be idle or
worse to recall it. Well ! she was not striving to

recall it; she was only going to act on the good old
medical suggestion of "taking a hair of the dog
that had bitten her." The romance was over—and
there had never been any romance—and she wasn't
wanting to recall it—and yet why shouldn't she
wish to recall all that there had been? Absence
disillusions most women, but the disillusioning is
the fruit of certain conditions. They have no time
to think of the absent one, if they have some one
else present. She had been oppressed with too
much idle time for the last eighteen months, and
she had seen no man capable of displacing Walter
Goring from his pedestal. Faithfulness in the
case of the unbound very often is but a shallow
euphemism for lack of opportunity.

CHAPTER XIV.

RELEASED.

WHEN her brother Frank and Walter Goring went away together, the dead calm that succeeded the lately tempestuous moral atmosphere was a hard thing to live through gracefully. Charlie could not help marvelling sometimes whether she had indeed been born for no other end than this, that she might make things as pleasant as possible to a man who made things uncommonly unpleasant to her. One half of her time was spent now in being ashamed for him, and the other half in being afraid for him. Whenever he was away from her she feared a repetition of that stumbling performance when he had gone over the old brown hunter's head; and when he was with her he brought the blushes to her face with such fell frequency, that wifely feeling was pretty well burnt out.

People who "knew" them still, who recognised
the existence of the Fellowes', though they were of
The Hurst no longer, in a gracious and merciful
manner that was infinitely more disgusting than any
amount of obliviousness would have been—these
people said, "how well he bore his reverses," and
what " a comfort it must be to her that her husband
didn't give way to low, spirits," thus making it
patent that the air he adopted abroad was one of
offensive jollity.   They little knew his black moodiness at home.   The moodiness that made almost a
tangible cloud in the house, and that knew no
shadow of a change save into maudlin self-pity.   It
was very hard for her to live under it; to feel that
her youth was passing away under it.   Very, very
hard to feel that she had none other than herself to
thank for it.   The memory of the manner in which
she had accepted this man's offer of marriage, back
(*how* far back it seemed) in the pretty road near
Portslade, was always with her.   The recollection
of the honest feeling against accepting it which she
had crushed and put away from her, because, oh,
fool ! she had yearned for any change—would not be
banished.   It was very hard, but the punishment
was less than the offence, so she would go on re-

adjusting her burden and trying to walk with her head up under it.

There was such an absence of every element of diversion in her life. The dull little country town in which she lived, the dreary women with whom she dwelt, were very stagnating in their influence. She had no friends, no society, no amusement save books and—old memories. She was as badly placed as a woman with a quick imagination can be placed; it was surely some slight merit in her, that under it all she kept a bright face, and struggled to think that her lot was quite as good as she deserved or— desired.

She wrote constantly now—when her husband was not rabid in his claims on her attention—and she had succeeded (or her publishers had succeeded for her) in making a little bit of a name. But it was the pursuit of literature under difficulties. Now that Frank, and that other one who knew what she meant always without her needing to give wordy explanations,—now that they were away, the saving interest, the helping sympathy, the encouraging word, which we all need, were each and all lacking. Her husband had a vague kind of notion, to which he would give utterance sometimes in a vague kind

of way, that it was her romance-writing which had
weaned her from him, and inclined her to another
—as he could not but see that she did incline. But
she might have replied to this charge in L. E. L's.
tinkling words :

> " It was not my loved lute," she said,
> "My gentle lute, that wrought the wrong ;
> It was not song that taught me love ;
> But it was love that taught me song."

But he, as people are very apt to do, made confusion
between cause and effect.

At last she was deprived of even the poor diversion of making pleasant and miserable the lives of
imaginary people. Henry Fellowes fell ill from
cold and other causes, and then the hardest, sad-
dest duties of a wife were laid upon her, and everything gave way before the great necessity of nursing
him through a long wearying sickness.

For six months the days rolled along with no
shadow of a change, at least with none greater than
his being a little better one day and much worse the
next. A terrible time, for he was more exacting
than ever ; he would take nothing save from her
hand, and he would not suffer her to be five minutes
out of his presence. He did not like her to read—

the very thought of her writing threw him into such
a state of irritable agitation the first week of his
being confined to his bed, that she locked up her
desk, and promised him that until he was quite
well she would not open it again. From that time
she sat through the days in that darkened room,
never moving save to serve him, with no other
object than to soothe and ease one of the most frac-
tious patients it ever fell to a woman's lot to tend.

She never seemed to weary over her task; he
grew more satisfied with her every day—more
satisfied, that is to say, that she was loving him at
last,—in which, poor fellow, he was mistaken. She
was not loving him; she was only feeling more and
more sorry for him because she could not love him,
now that he was so ill and helpless and dependent
on her. The knowledge that she could not do it
made her tender, with a tenderness that was as
watchful, patient and long-suffering as love itself
could have been; it gave her the indomitable
courage to endure, which love alone is popularly
supposed to give. It sustained her as the days
rolled into weeks, and the weeks into months, and
the once strong hale man became more and more
attenuated, more and more helpless, more and more

hollow-eyed and sunken-cheeked, and, alas! more and more fractiously exacting. That tenderness and the feeling, half pity, half remorse, from which it sprang, enabled her to keep up, in a way that made her mother-in-law marvel at her, and acknowledge to the doctor that "Henry might have done worse." It carried her through darksome, hopeless days, when he was so very ill that it was only through the hold he kept of her hand—the little hand whose light fine touch was the only one he could bear—that she knew he was asleep, *not* dead. It carried her through sleepless nights of bending over his pillow, when he could not bear her to be even so far away from him as the little sofa at the other end of the room. It carried her, in fact, bravely through as sad and fatiguing a half year as can well be imagined. And at the end of the six months it deepened, and the feelings from whence it sprang deepened too, when her task was brought to a conclusion by her husband's death.

This was the reason which Frank St. John had for coming home—his sister was alone in the world in reality; and perhaps this was the reason Walter Goring had for remaining away.

For some three or four months after Henry

Fellowes' death, Charlie remained with his mother and sister. Strangely enough, they seemed to cling to her now; they had a jealousy of her leaving them. It was not even pleasant to them to hear that Frank was coming home to take his sister to live with him. So Charlie, as a still further faint sort of expiation for the never-forgotten wrong she had done her husband in marrying him without love, promised to stay with them as long as they willed it, gave up the happy prospect of a home in London with Frank—of Frank's bright companionship and aid, and promised to remain in the atmosphere that she could not alter her nature sufficiently to find congenial. It was about this time, just as she had promised to stay with them, that Mrs. Walsh came back to Deneham, and then, among other pleasing and diverting topics of conversation that kindly callers indulged in, was the probability—which they discussed freely—of Mr. Goring coming home, and marrying his beautiful tenant.

There was very little intercourse between the two widows. They went occasionally, and sat the orthodox ten minutes in each other's houses; but Mrs. Walsh's was the well-endowed and refined country life, and, to tell the truth, Charlie did not

like to contrast it with her own.   Mrs. Walsh lived
in a cottage, but it was a cottage that stood on a
sloping lawn, in the centre of which beds of the
fairest flowers, geometrically arranged, made a gorgeous mosaic.   It was a cottage the pretty low
walls of whose rooms were hung with delicately-
tinted satin-surfaced papers, against the pale green
and grey of which gilt frames and good bronzes
stood out magnificently.   It was a cottage where
the simple latticed windows were hung with rose-
coloured or crimson silk curtains, which threw
good marble copies of the best antique sculptures
into fair relief.   It was a cottage that was always
pervaded with the perfume of fresh flowers—that
was always as trim, and perfectly appointed and
delicately ordered as money alone permits a house
to be.   Small wonder that Charlie, whose taste was
much towards similar things, should eschew contrasting it with her dwelling-place.

The great London beauty was living an idyll.
She would not respond to the advances the county
people made to her, simply because she knew that
it was upon the cards that at the expiration of her
lease she might see cause to remove herself from
the neighbourhood, and it was useless to get in with

a lot of people for so short a time. But though she did not visit, and though Walter Goring was away, she was not at all dull. "I hold it true, whate'er befall," that one never can be dull if left to oneself with beautiful inanimate things about one, plenty of books to read, and nice horses to ride and drive. Mrs. Walsh was surrounded by these conditions of successful solitude. Her eye was always pleased when she was in her house; the things were her own, and were dear to her by association. Things of beauty that do not belong to one are not half so satisfactory. And when she was out of the house, she was fain to confess that the Norfolk roads may not easily be surpassed for riding and driving purposes.

There was a certain pleasure too—besides the mere fact of driving her handsome chestnut cobs—in going over the ground once more which she had gone over with Walter Goring on the occasion of her first visit to Goring Place. How merrily the days had spun by then, to be sure, when they had bowled over the ground in Walter's trap, she up in front with him, and that poor dead Daisy behind with Mr. Levinge! As she went along the roads sometimes, she felt that, surely, though two of the *dramatis personæ* were gone beyond the bourne from whence there is no return, that the two who were left would see the old places together again. Here at Walsingham Abbey they had all four of them knelt laughingly at the "Wishing Well," and drank and wished in that bright unclouded August weather when she saw the place first. It was August again now—three years after—as she stood by the well alone, having left her cobs and man down in the village. Had any of their wishes come true? None! None! The Daisy had not wished for crossed love and early death, assuredly, when she had bent down with her yellow hair floating behind her, and drank of the crystal water. Was it worth going on and evoking other memories by visiting some of the other shrines to which they had made pilgrimages? No, certainly not.

It rarely is worth while to harrow up one's own feelings by recalling old memories. These latter are pretty in poetry, and fascinating in fiction, but they are generally intolerable in real life. There almost invariably appears to be a touch less of pleasantness (to say the least of it) in the present than the past. Three years is a long time in a woman's life. It is impossible for her to avoid contrasting her looks then and now when she glances back through the vista. She was paler, or more pinky, better rounded, or more sylph-like, in the bemoaned by-gone she remembers. The intervening years have witnessed the dissolution of some friendships and some hopes that made life a little brighter while they lasted. On the whole, resuscitations are always obnoxious and to be avoided. Nevertheless, in her case, alive as she was to the propriety of forgetting, the dead days would not quite bury their dead. Her memory was unfortunately green.

When she was well out on the road once more passing along between the close, regularly clipped hedges, what innumerable old associations leapt out upon her from either side! There, at the sharp turn, where one of the drives from a pretty manor-house gleaming white among the trees ran down into a point and joined the road, the trap had swerved, and Daisy had been nearly off. She remembered now how she had not condescended to look round and ascertain the amount of damage done, though Daisy had given a well-modulated scream. The road was unaltered—there was precisely the same tint upon the trees now as then,

the same degree of warmth in the air, the same
sounds from the harvestmen in the fields ; but she
herself was three years older than she had been
then, and Daisy was dead !

Somehow or other, a feeling of depression came
over her. " You nice county that has been brushed
and combed into almost beauty, you won't be my
abiding-place ! " she thought, half shaking her head
at the landscape as she passed along it. " ' Few
views worth painting about here ! ' poor Ralph said
once. How is it that so many of them have painted
themselves on my heart, I wonder ? I suppose it
would be the same with any place I knew with Walter
Goring ; he has the art of making things pleasant.
Absurd of me, at *my* age, to be undergoing the
' Wherever thou art would seem Erin to me ' sensations ! " Then she whipped her cobs, and tried
to forget him ; and went on remembering vividly
that he had been wont to call her " his goddess,"
and that young Mrs. Fellowes was free as well as
herself.

CHAPTER XV.

FRANK ST. JOHN did not receive the announcement of his sister's determination, to stay with the
family of her late husband so long as they needed
her, at all well. He had given up a life that suited
him, pursuits that pleased him, and the companionship of a man whom he liked very much, in order to
come back to make a home for Charlie. And now
Charlie made all this null and void out of some absurd scruples. "I'll wait and see the book out, and
then I will go back to Goring," he said, but by the
time the book was out, and he quite ready for the
start back to California, things arranged themselves
according to his first wishes. A gentleman who,
twenty years before, had been suspected of enter-
taining tender feelings towards Miss Dinah—having
tested himself and her by this sensible unhasting

gauge of waiting nearly a quarter of a century to see
whether anybody else intervened—suddenly took
heart of grace, and declared himself. Accordingly
Miss Dinah took him in holy matrimony, and her
mother to live with her. So Charlie was quite free
to go away at last, and live the life Frank had projected for her.

It must be acknowledged that Mrs. Walsh was
very glad to witness Charlie's exodus from Deneham. Not that Mrs. Walsh had jealous forebodings,
but she did not want things to remain undecided for
a week after Walter Goring came back, and Walter
Goring might come back any day, and Charlie might
have the effect of rendering him uncertain. So she
witnessed Charlie's exodus with pleasure, and hoped
heartily that Charlie would like her new London
life too well ever to come back to Deneham.

Both the brother and sister were thriving in
their respective walks of art. Frank drew for wood
engraving a good deal, and Charlie, considerably
elongated, was useful to him as a model very often
for those wonderful young ladies who adorn the
pages of our illustrated magazines, young ladies
who are all six feet high, and richly gifted with eyes
that are bigger than their mouths—and Charlie sold

her stories at fluctuating prices truly, but still sold them. The first thing they did, therefore, was to take a pretty little house in a western suburb, in what, in blind reliance on the agent's veracity, they believed to be a quiet neighbourhood. A semi-detached house in a road some little distance from the highway. A road in which willows wept, and ladies stood out on their little drawing-room balconies on summer evenings—and crickets chirped in a confiding way as darkness fell in a most anti-metropolitan manner. A road rendered respectable by a church all to itself at one end—and rendered something else (shall it be called interesting ?) by divers parrots in divers windows, shaded by the pinkest of curtains—by little dogs of snowy hue—by two or three retiring little broughams which were great at waiting—by miniature mail-phaetons and pairs that went out with a dash and came home with a limp. A little road in which the residents were almost exclusively of the gentler sex, and the visitors almost as exclusively of the other, through nature's great law of compensation.

" A sweet little road, close to the park, and quite near enough to Piccadilly, and yet so quiet—just the very place to work in," Charlie said to her brother,

in a burst of satisfaction with her new abode on the
night of their taking possession. She modified that
statement about its being the very place for working
in afterwards. From nine o'clock in the morning
till ten at night sons of harmony ground their
weary length along the quiet road. Italian boys
with monkeys found it a pleasant place wherein to
spend the noontide hour. On Monday it was the
favoured resort of a distressed father and five
dilapidated children, who sang their agonies in
jerks. On Tuesday a corresponding mother im-
parted an additional and purely maternal interest to
a similar performance. On Wednesday an ingenious
but unpleasant man made miserable melody by
rubbing his wretched wet fingers round the rims of
glasses arranged on a board. On Thursday the
whole of the above-mentioned had a grand field day,
and out-howled one another. On Friday a band of
German boys eased their tender hearts by playing
"Fatherland;" and on Saturday the agonies of the
week culminated in the Indian with his tom-tom.
The quiet little road was catholic in its musical
tastes, undoubtedly, but the general liberality of
sentiment on the subject was not of an order to
appeal to a working resident whose nerves were

on the surface, and who was conscious of a brain.

However, they had taken the house, and it behoved them to make the best of it. "Nice customs curtsey to great kings," but mere insignificant subjects are compelled very often to curtsey to nasty customs. In time Charlie got into a habit of enduring the Indian with his tom-tom—which is more like the toothache than anything else in this world; she even grew calm enough about him to contemplate the possibility of making copy out of him at some future time.

So time rolled on for about a year—then a break occurred. There had been some trifling business relating to the affairs of her late husband still unsettled when Charlie had left Deneham. Some house property in one of the adjacent parishes had fallen to the late Henry Omry Fellowes (as a lapsed legacy), or rather to the late Henry Omry Fellowes' widow and sole legatee. The houses were old, incommodious, and consequently ill-let, but the site on which they stood was good. A practical builder, with an eye for the picturesque, saw that it was so, and made specious advances towards purchasing them of Mrs. Fellowes, who, lacking the business mind, suffered these advances to drift away into nothing for a period of many months.

At last, on the occasion of receiving the small quarterly rents, it occurred to her to tell Frank that some man had wanted to buy on lease the land on which these unremunerative tenements stood for building purposes, and it was decided that whenever Frank should chance to find himself with a couple of days at his disposal that he should go down and see about making the best bargain he could for his sister.

"You'll have to stay a night or two down there, Frank," she suggested, when the spare days came in due course, and when he replied, "Yes," she added, "Then make Deneham your head-quarters, and just give a look at —— "

"Mrs. Walsh? Yes, certainly," he interrupted.

"I wasn't going to say Mrs. Walsh, but Goring Place," she laughed; "but if you should see your Guinevere, say something very civil from me."

It was late summer weather when Frank went on his business mission to Deneham, and it was settled that on his return Charlie and he should start for a tour they had long contemplated through the western counties. They had not organised a perfect plan of operations yet, but they had almost decided on avoiding railway-riddled tracks, and travelling in search of the picturesque on stout ponies,—their luggage to be sent on to certain salient points here·after to be fixed upon, and they themselves to be quite free to vagabondise for a month, unfettered by all time-table considerations.

This prospect had a great charm for both the brother and sister. They had had a long spell of uninterrupted hard work, and they both felt that it would be good for them in their respective arts to lie fallow for a time—to get away out of the atmo-sphere of publishing and picture-dealing, of reviews and reviewers—to breathe an air unsullied by the sordid interest attaching to these things—to get out of the orbit of the daily papers, and the sound of the roar of the young lions thereof—to flee paint, pens, and paper, and not to give their address to anyone.

"Be ready to start on Friday, Charlie. We'll go right away down to Dawlish at once, and cruise about from there for a few days," Frank said to his sister, when he was leaving for Deneham on the Tues-day morning. So, during the two or three days of his absence, Charlie looked forward to preparing

travelling-dresses that should stand any weather and
much wear for a month—dresses in which she could
mount a pony without looking ridiculous, and which
would still be suitable for walking on the earth in.

Meanwhile Frank had gone down and settled the
building business, and had made a duty call on
Mrs. Foster, late Miss Dinah Fellowes, and a
pleasure call on Mrs. Walsh, who gave him that sort
of welcome a woman does accord the friend of the
man she is most interested in, when that man is
absent, and the friend has seen him long since she
herself has.

"I was up in town for a few days in June, Mr. St.
John," she said to him, "and I saw your picture in
the Academy."

"Which one?" he asked, "'A Turning Point'
or 'A Falling Star?'—the second is a sequel to the
first."

"I only saw the 'Turning Point,' and I liked the
feeling with which you indicated a terrible story;
there was great tenderness in it, and great truth."

Frank felt his face flushing with pleasure; his
fair critic's husband had been a great painter, and
had taught her to discriminate—must have taught
her to discriminate.   He felt very much flattered.

"Did you ever chance to see my Guinevere?" he asked, presently.

She shook her head.

"Never; long ago before you had nearly finished it, Walter Goring and I walked up to your studio—in Sloane Street you were then—to look at it, but you were out, and the door was locked."

"You know it is at Goring Place?" he said, interrogatively.

"I did not know it. Had I known it, I should have gone to see it long long ago; for I *did* hear, Mr. St. John, that you paid me the compliment of introducing a very flattering portrait of me in it."

"Will you come and see it now, Mrs. Walsh?" he asked, eagerly; "do let me show it to you. It was my first work, and now after three years incessant study and labour, I should like to learn from your remarks on it whether I have made any headway in my art or not."

She grew rather pale at the idea of going to Goring Place with another than the master of it. There was a touch more pain than pleasure in the prospect of doing so. Such trifles chill and sting a woman when the course of a love that she fancies

true does not run smooth. Still she desired to
please and encourage the man who, though he was
her rival's brother, was her lover's friend.

" Then we'll drive over at once. I have never
been inside the gates since Walter left. There are
few things more unpleasant to me than going alone
to a deserted place where I have once been very
happy, if not gay."

"If it will give you pain——"

" It will not, to go with you," she interrupted,
smiling. "I spoke of going alone." Then she
rang the bell and ordered her pony-carriage, and
shortly after scandalised and excited the worst
feelings of Deneham by driving the handsome
stranger through its streets.

It is a very dubious and a very ghastly pleasure
after all, going to the deserted home of one who is
dear to you. There is a sense of blankness and
desolation about the unused rooms that induces
melancholy reflection in the most vivacious and
least reflective. Half the furniture is shrouded in
chilling linen and the other half in dust. Black-
beetles and other monsters which in inhabited
days were only to be found in the " vasty deep " of
the cellars, advance upon you from unsuspected

corners, and "rise up on their hind-legs, gnashing their teeth upon you" and obliging you
to skip, in order to avoid crushing them, in
a way that causes you to feel a forlorn and
foolish wanderer in insect and old memory-
haunted wilds. All things that have not taken
the damp have taken the dry-rot, and the rest
are rusty and broken. The piano is out of tune,
and so are you. There is too much reverberation
and too much echo, and too much contrast between
what has been and what is, altogether for sadness
not to obtain a temporary dominion.

When Mrs. Walsh pulled up her ponies at the
lodge-gates, the first sign of the marked difference
they were soon to see more fully, smote upon both
Frank and herself. Instead of the speedy orderly
opening of other days, when a smart young woman
(the under-gardener's wife) had always held herself
in readiness to swing open the gates at the first
sound of the approach of her master or his guests;
—instead of this prompt portress, a little child
pattered out of the lodge—gazed at them with an
expression of pleased amaze in its wide blue eyes—
advanced gallantly upon the gate, and then, instead
of opening it, strove to insert its broad chubby feet

between the bars, for the purpose of clambering up and more fully examining the invaders.

"Open the gate, my little fellow!" Frank shouted; but instead of opening the gate the child made a shrill appeal to its "mammy" to come out; and then a strange woman came through the doorway and demanded, rather insolently, whether they had a pass for the park, as she couldn't let them in without it. "Mr. Goring don't wish it showed," she continued, turning about as if to go into the lodge again. Then Frank parleyed with her in a high key, much to his own indignation, and finally they were admitted, half on sufferance as it seemed.

"Seeing my Guinevere won't repay you for all this bother and annoyance, Mrs. Walsh," Frank said, in a vexed tone, as they drove through the gate-way at last; and Mrs. Walsh gave her chestnuts a fierce little cut which betrayed that she had felt being made to wait.

"I think it will more than repay me; considering my vanity will find balm in the sight of myself idealised."

"I had no occasion to idealise. I wanted 'beauty such as never woman wore,' and I found it."

A blush so slight that it might only have been the effect of the sun, covered her face as he spoke. Then she flicked her ponies again, but not fiercely at all this time, and said,—

"But you had only seen me once, Mr. St. John, had you?"

"I had only seen you once; but I never forgot a line of your face. I knew the pencilling by heart, from the moment I first saw you, so well, that at any time during these three years I could have painted your portrait from memory, and made it a vivid likeness."

She looked him frankly in the face, and said,—

"I am very much flattered."

"You! flattered by anything I can say?"

"I am very, very much flattered by your——"

"Admiration," he interrupted. "I can't express to you how strong it is. I never thought that I should have dared to try to express it. No one knows the depth of it, save Walter: he called you my inspiration."

The blush burnt more brightly on her face, as Frank poured the sentence out rapidly. "Walter knew it and didn't disapprove of it," she thought; "on the contrary, he rather fostered it by giving it a

fine name. I dreamt of being Walter's inspiration
once. What a glorious face this Frank St. John
has—as fair, frank and proud as Apollo's."

They had come, by the time her thoughts reached
this point, to the gravel-sweep in front of the house.
The gardens showed the absence of their owner.
The bedding-out plants had not been bedded-out;
the croquet-ground no longer looked like green
velvet; and a raggedly grown untrimmed Westeria
in splendid bloom drooped down, entirely concealing
the windows of the drawing-room, where poor Daisy
had broken the cabinet and claimed the picture,
and where afterwards Mrs. Walsh had been introduced by Walter to his wilful, wayward, charming
ward.

They had to go through this room, when after a
little more delay they were admitted into the house,
in order to gain that small room where the picture
had been hung. As they approached it Frank felt
the old sensations of sorrow and remorse that his
should have been the hand to discover Daisy's
falseness to Walter and love for Levinge, which had
oppressed him that night when the poor little girl
had stood braving them all at bay.

"You know the story, don't you?" he asked in

a low voice, when they came at last before the
picture, and Mrs. Walsh started and exclaimed at
sight of the " Lancelot and Elaine,"—

" Mr. Levinge and Daisy ! No, I don't know it.
Walter wrote me word that his marriage with his
cousin was broken off, and that she was engaged to
Levinge. But he offered no explanation, and I
asked for none."

" They are both dead now. The truth can't hurt
them," Frank said, mournfully. So then, standing
before the picture, he told the story, and Mrs. Walsh
found herself far more affected than she once
deemed she could have been at aught concerning
Daisy.

" Has it ever been found out who her mother was,
and why Daisy made a mystery about her ? " she
asked, wiping her eyes as she went and sat down
before the Guinevere.

" Making the mystery was one of her weaknesses.
Yes, we found that her mother had been a concert-
singer—not a famous one by any means—when old
Goring knew her. He wronged her, as you know,"
he continued, hurriedly, " and then forgot all about
her, as it seems. Two or three years afterwards a
man, a clergyman, fell in love with and married her,

on condition she quitted the boards entirely, and she consented to marry him on condition of being allowed to retain Daisy, whom she passed off as her niece, the child of a dead sister. After fifteen or sixteen years' marriage, the scruples of her sex assailed her. She gave herself up; she betrayed her former lover, and she forfeited her child to her husband's wrath. She had never been wicked you see, Mrs. Walsh, but she was weak as water."

"And Walter would have married the daughter of that woman!" Mrs. Walsh exclaimed; "a woman who could sin and repent for the sake of gaining a mediocre establishment, and who ended by sacrificing the man for whom she had sacrificed herself! It's a pitiful story."

"It would have been but for Daisy," Frank said, stoutly; "there was nothing pitiful in Daisy's share in it: she would never have married Goring, even if that daub had not made the truth manifest when it did. Poor little creature! I shall never forget her standing there fronting us all, trying not to quail at the sight of Walter's sorrow, for fear we should think she was ashamed of her love for Levinge."

"Was Walter so very sorrowful about it?"

" He was. What man wouldn't have been ? " Frank cried, heartily.

"Yours was the worst position. You were so blameless and so miserably placed; *you* to play the part of domestic detective, however undesignedly !"

" It was undesignedly—heaven knows ! You know that, don't you ? "

" Do I not ? Indeed I do so well. What a lot of pain there is in life," she continued, sadly.

" But each pang has its compensating pleasure."

"I don't think so : instance yourself, Mr. St. John. What compensation can you ever find for the pang of having been the cause of that disclosure ? We can't be too thankful for Walter's sake that it was made when it was; it enabled him to try to make that poor girl happy. But what can compensate you for the pain of being the cause ? "

" Your sympathy—that compensates me."

" Such a poor trifle ! does it ? "

She looked so bravely up at him as she spoke, and she was so very beautiful. " By Jove ! I wish I hadn't come," he thought; "I was very well before ;—ass that I was not to know how it would be if I came down and saw more of her."

" Shall we go away now ? " she asked, presently,

in a low voice, and he assented to her proposition, though he hated going away. He seemed to have a nearer interest in her standing there before that semblance of herself which he had painted.

The thing he liked next best to her exceeding beauty in this woman was, that she was not piously anxious to draw morals and adorn tales from Daisy's story. The little blonde who had looked upon that picture of his, and known herself a found-out fallen star, had sinned doubtless; but had she not suffered—suffered unto death? He would have loathed any untempted woman who had sat in judgment upon her—he would have deemed any woman weak who had for effect seemed to seek to find commonplace excuses for the girl who had been consumed by her ill-placed passion. But Mrs. Walsh did not seek to extenuate, nor did she set down aught in malice. She just accepted the facts of Daisy's case, and found them sad; but she did not strive to improve them for the edification of the living.

He liked this quality in her—ah! and how many others?

> " A thing of beauty is a joy for ever,
>   It's loveliness increases ; it will never
>   Pass into nothingness."

So he sang who touched the beautiful mythology of Greece, and did *not* " dim its brightness," and so he believed probably when he wrote the opening lines of his " Endymion." But Frank St. John knew better, or thought he knew better. The beauty of this woman now looking up into his face would cease to be a joy to him, did it pass—not into " nothingness," but into the possession of Walter Goring. " I shall never be able to stand it," he thought; " I shall leave dear little Charlie to fight her way by herself, and cut my native land. Fancy the fellow who could come home and have *her*— staying away in California !" There was the law of compensation at work even here. Walter evidently had not the joyful power of fully appreciating the glory that had befallen him in having gained this woman's tenderest smiles.

" Shall we walk round the house ? " she asked at last, and then they made their way to the room wherein Daisy used to sing with Laurence Levinge. The room was the same ; not a tint of its delicate green was faded ; no blur had come over the surface of the gold on moulding and picture-frame. The same spider-legged little tables stood about to upset the unwary ; the same untarnished mirrors flashed back your face when you looked into them; the same myrtle which *she* had planted bloomed and budded in the jardinière; the same low couch on which Mrs. Walsh had sat, with Walter at her side, on the night of her first arrival at Goring Place, stretched its luxurious expanse; the same winking Cupid on the ormolu clock on the mantle-board levelled his golden arrows at the hour and half-hour; but the piano was silent, and Daisy was dead.

The room was ghastly in its unaltered state. Whether it had been through mere carelessness, or through some half-unconscious sentiment on the part of the housekeeper, they could not tell. They could only feel that it was all painfully as of old.

There on the centre table—open still, and turned down on the face of its pages—was that volume of Macaulay's lays which Daisy had been reading when Walter took her away to Brighton first, when his own educational code had failed. It was such a little thing to touch them. Probably the book had been taken up scores of times since Daisy put it down; taken up and dusted, and carefully readjusted by some housemaid's hand. But for all this probability it seemed to be so very sacred to the fair

dead girl who had opened it at that page. It was
such a very little thing to touch them, but somehow
or other they were touched by it, or something else
which I cannot define.

Briefly, but very kindly, as they were afterwards
walking through the picture gallery which Ralph
Walsh had rearranged, did Mrs. Walsh allude to
her husband. " There was no method observed,
and every picture was hung in the worst light
when we came down here to stay ; now the true
artist's hand is traced in the placing of each one.
Don't you see it ? "

" They're hung as well as they could be hung on
such walls ; these deeply-embrasured windows are
not the ones to show off pictures to advantage."

" Well, no, they're not; but my husband did all
that could be done. It was the last exercise of
his great talent—the better adornment of Walter
Goring's house."

She smiled almost tenderly as she spoke, and
Frank waxed uncomfortable. Allusions, fond allusions to Walter, friend though Walter was of
Frank's, were not too pleasant things to which to
listen. But this linking together of the "loved lost
and the loved living" was specially distasteful.

"It all falls to Walter's share," Frank said, after a brief space.

" All what ? "

"Friendship, fortune, success, love—everything that makes life worth having, in fact."

"Has he availed himself of it all ? Does he seem as if he cared for the friendship ? He *knows* our hearts are wrung with anxiety for him, yet he stays away in those horrid wilds from choice."

She spoke in a sudden gust of affectionate indignation; she could not resist betraying the chagrin she felt at this perversity of my hero's. Frank could not sympathise with her.

"I must acknowledge that my heart isn't much wrung with anxiety about Walter. It's not half so savage as you're pleased to suppose : he has his rifles and dogs, and two or three Mexican servants with him."

"Oh, I don't doubt his capability of taking care of himself," she replied, with her sex's inconsistency. "Shall we go away now ? It's rather depressing, walking about these deserted halls."

As they were driving home, Mrs. Walsh asked, " Have you seen your sister ? "

"I saw her the day I left, of course," he answered. To him, there was but one sister in the world—Charlie.

"Ah! I meant your other sister, Mrs. Prescott."

"No; are they at the Hurst?"

"Oh, yes; and you must go and see them," she replied, wheeling her cobs round rather too sharply into the re-opened private lane that led from Goring Place to the Hurst. The sudden swerve excited the chestnuts; they made a sharp bolt forward before the hind-wheels of the phaeton could turn; the bricked corner of the hedge came crashing against them; the cobs started off at full speed, and in an instant or two the phaeton went over the near side, and Mrs. Walsh and Frank were both shot out.

CHAPTER XVI.

" THANK the Lord, it's the left arm," Frank
thought, when he had picked himself up and discovered that the limb of which he spoke stood off
from the elbow at an acute and unnatural angle.
He had seen immediately that Mrs. Walsh was un-
hurt, or he would not have thought an adjuration
about himself at all.

The cobs had kicked themselves free of the pole ;
and they now stood panting, with their traces hanging
loosely about them, and the buttoned boy, who
always accompanied Mrs. Walsh, at their heads.
That youth stood very much agape when his ordinarily composed mistress reproached herself and
her chestnuts and her page as the cause of the
accident to Mr. St. John, all in one breath. "My
awkwardness ! They are full of vice from want of

work! Why didn't you take Robin Hood up a hole or two before we started, John?" she continued, angrily alluding to the pony that had been in on the near side, and who had, to tell the truth, evinced a marked inclination to shirk his work and play at going breadth-ways several times. "Mr. St. John, what can I—*what can* I do?"

Frank's arm was swelling rapidly. It was a promising dislocation at the elbow; the small bone was broken immediately below it, and the wrist was sprained. Altogether the accident was a remarkably complete one.

"I tell you what I'll do. Trust me to pull your arm in—I can!"

He saw that her face flushed as she spoke. He would have distrusted the pulling-in powers of a woman who had gone pale while proposing it. "Trust you! I'd trust you to do that or anything else," he replied; "but you haven't the strength." Then he tried a feeble smile, and added, "When men get out of joint, they don't go in again in a hurry."

"Let me try—do let me try!" she cried. "Have you a knife?"

He had a knife, very much at her service.

Accordingly, she ripped his coat-sleeve from the wrist to the shoulder-seam; cut open his shirt-sleeve very daintily, and then without the shadow of a tremble prepared to pull in the swollen limb which she had been the cause of dislocating.

All round the region of the elbow-joint the flesh had puffed up terribly. She shuddered inwardly when she saw it, but she would not suffer the shudder to make itself visible. "Put your arm round my waist to steady yourself. I'll be like a rock, Mr. St. John," she said, when she laid her long, snowy-white fingers on the battered wrist; and, tender as her touch was, it seared his tortured flesh like hot iron. The next moment there was a creaking and a horrible jerk, and—the joint was rightly adjusted again. No one who has not had his elbow dislocated can quite appreciate the profound intensity of that love of the beautiful which enabled Frank to think only of the grace and charm with which Mrs. Walsh performed this little bit of surgery while she was doing it.

When she had made a temporary sling out of the silk scarf she wore, there was nothing else to be done save to get home and send for a doctor as soon as possible. Mrs. Walsh wanted to send her boy into Deneham for a carriage, but Frank declared himself able to walk.

"I must drop a line to Charlie," he said, "or she'll be wild on Friday if I don't put in an appearance; and I don't think I'll risk a railway journey on the Great Eastern yet."

"I should think not. I will write to Mrs. Fellowes, and beg her to come down, Mr. St. John. You must stay at my house till you have quite got over the effect of my carelessness."

Frank St. John tried very hard to refuse this invitation with manly firmness and decision. He knew well that it would only be the worse for him eventually if he did put himself in the way of seeing her constantly. But she routed every excuse he made, and finally he gave way and consented to go and be happy for a time under her roof, and to be in diurnal receipt of her tender sympathy.

"She does it for Walter's sake," he thought; "I'm Walter's friend. No doubt she'd nurse a dog of his just as tenderly. Well, it's my luck—it's this child's destiny. 'No woman's eyes shall smile on me, no woman's heart be mine,' I suppose. I hope Ellen won't come over and bother me to go to The Hurst, though there'll be more pain than pleasure very likely in staying with Mrs. Walsh, especially when the edge of her admiration for him is whetted by the sight of Charlie. But I'll be a Christian martyr, and bear my share of pain."

The doctor came, and found his task made comparatively easy through the prompt measures Mrs. Walsh had taken. He advised that Frank should go to bed at once, and sent him a sleeping draught. Frank took neither the advice nor the liquid composure; he sat in the drawing-room till eleven o'clock, and was made much of by Mrs. Walsh in a way that was far more soothing to his feelings. In order to retain this state of things he would not have had the smallest objection to dislocating each one of his limbs in succession; he blessed those swerving ponies and that obtrusive corner, and thought kind things of the boy who had neglected to take Robin Hood's traces up a hole or two. Finally he went to bed at eleven very much in love, and very conscious of his folly in being so. The consequence was that he passed a feverish night, and in the morning was found by his attendant to have vague notions about the majority of things. This grew, until by the time Charlie arrived (which she did late on the day following the accident) he was delirious, and Mrs. Walsh unfeignedly frightened.

Women almost invariably meet each other graciously in times of sickness. The hostess and her guest had been rivals—undiscovered rivals ; nevertheless now that they had this common interest they seemed to banish all memory of that rivalship, and to incline towards one another as sisters might have done, or rather as sisters are supposed to do by those of limitless faith, but do not too frequently.

Frank's was a very brief access of delirium, that is to say, he only stayed " out of his head " as the domestics of Mrs. Walsh's establishment termed it, for a day and a night. But the time, all brief as it was, had been quite long enough for him to commit himself to the statement of sundry sentiments which were quite new to his sister Charlie. They were new in verbal form also to Mrs. Walsh (who heard some of them very undesignedly in the course of sundry missions of mercy and assistance which she paid the sick-room), but that they were utterly unsuspected by that matron, after those passages before the pictures, is more than can be stated in truth.

Charlie had brought down all the letters which

had arrived for Frank since his departure, and among them was one from Walter Goring. "It has the San Francisco postmark upon it. He has evidently left the wilds and has come down to San Francisco; perhaps is on his way home," Charlie said, as Mrs. Walsh and herself stood investigating the envelope of the letter late at night.

"How very glad your brother will be to see him home again." Mrs. Walsh remarked in reply.

"Yes, and how his return will improve your neighbourhood."

"I don't suppose he will be here much—just in the hunting and shooting season. But there'll be too many claims on him in town for him to reside here altogether."

"Well, you know him much better than I do," Charlie said, with a spasm of pain at the truth of her own words. "You're far better able to judge of what he will do than I am."

"I have known him years—*how* many years longer—but *do* I know him better, Mrs. Fellowes?"

"I think you do," Charlie replied, frankly.

"I think I do not." Mrs. Walsh said, with equal

frankness. " I thought I knew him well,—knew him
as well as I loved him, until he wanted to marry
Daisy; that staggered my own faith in my knowledge
of his character : she was unsuited to him in every
way."

" Do you think that the consideration of suitable-
ness enters into people's calculations when circumstances bring about their marriage ? " Charlie
asked.

Mr. Walsh remembered Charlie's marriage and
her own, and declined to give a decided opinion.

"Because I don't," the embyro philosopher went
on. "What men think about chiefly, I can't say ;
pleasing themselves, I suppose. But the majority
of young women think about everything save those
contrasting or sympathetic points in a man's character which are essential to happiness in a close
union. My own idea now is that if I couldn't take
extreme pleasure in a man's society and companionship under any circumstances, that sense and
decency demand that I should utterly put down
the possibility of marrying him. This may seem
a very mild statement of feeling till you think about
it, Mrs. Walsh ; but when you *do* think about it,
say, how many girls are actuated by it after all ? Girls

take as their husbands men with whom they would
ridicule the idea of forming intimate friendships.
I *know* it."

"But on the other hand, how many intimate
friendships we form with men whom we wouldn't
marry on any consideration?"

"Yes—and that's redeeming, I allow; but my
proposition has a great deal too much truth about
it, you'll find, when you come to consider. Now I
must go to Frank."

"Let me sit up with you. What sorrow and
trouble I have been the means of causing you!"

"Yes you have," Charlie thought, "but not in
the precise way in which you mean it." Then she
thanked Mrs. Walsh for her offer of sharing the
vigil, and refused it, and went away with Walter's
letter in her hand to Frank's bedside.

The next morning Frank was better; well enough
to break the seal and read his letter and tell them
coherently that Walter announced his return. "We
are to expect him by the next mail—not the next,
the one after, unless he's delayed," Frank said in
the reverse of enthusiastic tones to his sister; then
Charlie passed the news along to Mrs. Walsh, and
the two women out of the intensity of their ner-

vousness grew almost affectionate to one another while discussing it.

Ellen came over as Frank had dreaded, and was anxious in a sisterly way about him. "I should like to see him, if he's not bruised in the face, Charlie," she said, after greeting the young widow.

" He's not bruised in the face, I assure you ; but if you have any doubts about your own nerves, don't go in : he's suffering too much to be disturbed by other people's emotions."

"I don't so much mind what he suffers if it doesn't show," Ellen replied, candidly.

" How consistent you are, Ellen ; always the same, dear. I would venture to stake my life on what your expressed feelings would be whenever you heard of anybody being hurt or injured."

Ellen bridled her fair pretty little head with pleasure. "Yes," she replied, "I always was dread-fully tender-hearted. I can't bear the sight of blood, or anything nasty. I daresay you don't mind it so much ; you always were a little coarser in your tastes. But really it is fortunate for Frank that you don't mind, isn't it ? "

"Perhaps it is. Well, come in, Ellen. But mind

I'll turn you out the instant you air your delicacy
of feeling. I won't have Frank agitated."

Mrs. Prescott was very far from being cold-hearted
or ill-natured. These are black qualities, and none
of hers were "put in" in anything but the most
undecided neutral tints. She was weak, that was
all; therefore, at the sight of Frank apparently
helpless in bed, she showered down a soft spray of
tears, and said "he *was* unfortunate, always unfortunate! dreadfully."

"Oh! this isn't so bad," he said, carelessly.
"How's Prescott?"

"Very well—in health," Ellen replied, as if her
husband were very ill in something else.

"Is he at The Hurst now?"

"Yes, he's there; you don't want anything of
him, do you, Frank?"

"I? No, certainly not."

"Ah, I'm so glad—I told him I didn't think you
would, but he was afraid your arm, you know,
might prevent your doing anything for a long time,
and it put him out: upset him."

"He's very good to be so considerate on Frank's
account," Charlie put in, rather haughtily.

"Yes, he is very good; I often think how lucky I

was to be settled and well provided for so young, while everything has gone wrong with you and Frank; it makes me quite wretched, quite low, when I think about you both often," Ellen continued, with that delightful vivacity people do occasionally display when discussing the sorrows of others. "There's Frank, now, no further on in life, and with not such good prospects as when he first went into the navy; and you have to *write* for your living, Charlie; it does seem hard."

"I think we've talked long enough to Frank now," Charlie interrupted.

"No," Frank said, laughing. "Ellen's sympathy is so uncommonly sweet that I'd like to have more of it."

"We think you might have found time to call at The Hurst, Frank," Mrs. Prescott resumed, suddenly adopting an injured tone. "You could go and see Mrs. Foster, and drive about with Mrs. Walsh, but your own sister you couldn't give an hour to. Don't you think Mrs. Walsh is falling off?"

"Not a bit," Charlie replied. She heartily wished that she could think Mrs. Walsh less beautiful than of yore, but it was not possible to do so.

"I suppose she's not likely to marry again—

unless she marries Mr. Goring, after all?" Ellen went on, meditatively.

"After all what?" Charlie questioned, sharply. The supposition was not a pleasant one for either Frank or herself, she felt.

"Why, after all you know; there's one thing certain, she can't marry unless the man has money."

"Why not?" Charlie was the speaker, Frank had turned his face rather more to the wall.

"Oh, because her husband made that a proviso. Mr. Prescott saw the will when he was in town last; if she marries again she loses her income."

"How unfair—how abominably unjust!" Charlie cried, indignantly.

"Mr. Prescott and I don't think so; *his* will is the same."

"I think I should like to have a sleep now, if you won't mind leaving me," Frank muttered, drowsily. Whereupon his sisters left him—to sleep?

No! not to sleep,—to think. Ellen was right. She had spoken a bitter truth in her feeble inconsiderate way when she said he was unlucky, and no further on in life than when he had gone into the navy a mere boy. Hope fled from his breast as he

recalled the past and pictured the future. He was
stung to the soul, and all energy was crushed out of
him.

Unconsciously he had nurtured the hope that
when Walter came home Charlie would reap her
reward, and win him, and that then Mrs. Walsh
might in time incline to another love. Frank had
determined to give Walter fair play. He would
take no mean advantage of his friend's absence, he
had told himself, but would just bide his time, and
if, when Walter came back, Charlie lost and his
Guinevere won, he (Frank) would accept his defeats
like a man. If, on the other hand, Walter Goring
gave unmistakeable evidence of its being only
friendship pure and simple which he had felt all
along for his Goddess, Frank would put his fate
to the touch, and seek her for his "wife" who had
been his "inspiration."

But now these resolves were broken up, sent to
the winds like chaff before the fell blast of Ellen's
tidings. For himself he did not want the money;
it would have been pleasant to have it together with
her of course, but it should have been under her
sole control. Nevertheless, though he did not want
the money, he felt that he could not ask her to for-

feit it by marrying him. Here, again, the gods
favoured Goring; *he* could make it up to her, what
she lost would be as nothing to what she would gain
in becoming the mistress of Goring Place. Luck
was against him in every way.

Lying there in a good deal of pain from his
broken arm, and a good deal more pain from his
broken hopes, his future looked a dreary dark blank
before him. "The many fail," in all things—
especially in all branches of art. "It was more
than probable that he was among the 'many'
destined to do so—it would only be like his luck.
Truly he had done tolerably well, had made good
progress heretofore, but it wouldn't last, nothing did
last with him. It was more than likely such creative
power as he had would fail him. Naturally the
public would get tired of his style. There were so
many better men than himself in the field that he
could only come in with the ruck. As it was, during
the period of his temporary popularity (he was convinced that it was only temporary) he would have to
waste his time and the little talent he had in doing
things that died with the day, and would never make
him a decent name. Whoever looked twice at the
pictorial part of a magazine? Or, indeed, for that

matter, whoever looked twice at any part of a magazine ? He wished from the bottom of his heart that
he had never written those essays in which he had
sought to prove the brilliantly original theory of
what is good in itself being acknowledged in time.
He had written them when he was in high spirits,
when he was happy, when the day was sufficient to
him, before he had seen so much of Mrs. Walsh, in
fact; and now they seemed like unto the brayings of
an idiotically contented and absurdly hopeful ass.
There was poor Charlie, too ! Wasn't her life one
unceasing struggle to seem happy and light-hearted,
when he knew very well that she wasn't so in reality ?
The whole thing was a big sham, and not worth
keeping up any longer ! " So things looked to him
in the morning. But in the evening they brightened.
John, the neglectful, who had omitted to take Robin
Hood up a hole or two, proved a capital valet.
Through his aid Frank inducted himself into his
clothes, and when he was dressed Mrs. Walsh sent
up a deputation in the person of Charlie to ask him
to come down into the drawing-room.

He went down, and his hostess met him at the
door, and drove the will and its consequences out of
his head by taking his sound hand in both her own

and welcoming him warmly. She was out of her
weeds, but she still wore black as a rule; this night,
however, " she regarded as a festival," she said, and
she had dressed for it accordingly. She was radiant
in her beauty, and her joy at seeing him down again,
and her white, soft, semi-transparent robe, girded in
round the waste with a silver cord. As Frank
looked at her and listened to her, he forgot his dark
doubts of the morning, and felt that he was safe to
do ever so much in the world, and to succeed
brilliantly.

It was very pleasant to play the invalid under
such auspices. Mrs. Walsh carried him his cup of
tea as he sat in one corner of the couch that was
generally sacred to herself; and she held the saucer
for him while he took the tea in slow sips, feasting
his eyes the while on her beauty, over the brim of
the cup. She also readjusted his sling for him.
Finally, she made a proposition which nearly sent
Frank off into delirium again.

The night was very lovely; daylight had not
quite died out of the sky yet, and as they sat near
to the open window the beauty of the evening and
the fact of Charlie having had no out-door exercise
that day struck Mrs. Walsh, who accordingly asked,

"Now wouldn't you like to go out for a drive, Mrs. Fellowes ? it would do you good."

" Frank's face fell ; he thought he was to be deserted ; but it brightened presently, when Mrs. Walsh added :

" John should drive you round to The Hurst and to see Mrs. Foster, if you liked. I will stay with Mr. St. John, and try not to let him feel dull while you're away."

Charlie hesitated, but Frank decided.

" I think you ought to go and see the late Miss Dinah, really, Charlie ; and the air will do you good, dear."

So Charlie went, and Frank and Mrs. Walsh were left alone together.

For five or six minutes after the little excitement of watching Charlie drive off, there settled a calm and a silence down upon them. Mrs. Walsh began to wish she had not proposed the drive ; Frank began to wish he had not seconded it. To what end, he asked himself, was a *tête-à-tête* vouchsafed to him when he could not in honour profit by it. Even if there had been no Walter Goring in the case, he could not ask a woman to give up liberty and plenty for penury and himself. The bare idea was preposterous; he could not be so mean—he could not be such a fool—he could not presume to reward her gracious condescension by such a piece of presumptuous madness.

His meditations were interrupted by her saying,

"Don't be offended with me, Mr. St. John, when I tell you that I'm perfectly surprised to see what a charming woman your sister has grown, or become rather."

"Do you think she has?" he replied.

He really could not take any intense interest in Charlie's development at the moment.

"Yes, very. I didn't like her at one time—I don't know why, but I did not—and she responded freely, I fancy; but we understand each other better now, and are very good friends. She is sure to marry again. You mustn't hope to keep her with you."

"I hope she will marry again; but I have heard her say that she never will."

"That means nothing," Mrs. Walsh said, quietly.

"In the majority of cases unquestionably it means nothing; but Charlie had a remarkably unpleasant experience, remember. She married a wealthy, jovial, manly, frank fellow, and in a few months he

turned out a bankrupt, drunken and ill-humoured.
I never said a word against my sister's husband
to anyone while he lived. I should never say what
I thought of him to her now, but I assure you, it
was the best news I had ever heard in my life when
I heard he was dead. She must have had an awful
time of it; not that she howled or complained—
she stood to her guns gallantly—but I know she
had an awful time of it."

"Yes; Walter Goring told me of one scene
which he witnessed the night of the auction at The
Hurst, the first time her husband stood a sot before
her."

"She has never told me of it," Frank said.

"Mr. Goring told me that the struggle between
her refinement and her sense of duty was an
agonising thing to witness; he was very much
impressed by it. I should have thought that she
was more likely to be swayed by feeling than anything else; but she didn't allow herself to be so in
that instance, Walter said."

"Her feelings always sway her in the right
direction," Frank said, fondly; "still though I
know that, I hope when I leave her that it will be
under a husband's protection."

" Leave her! Where are you going?"

"That I hardly know, myself, Mrs. Walsh. I only know that I must get away somewhere—because I dare not stay."

He spoke in an earnest, impassioned tone, fixing his eyes full on her face as he spoke. She was sitting on a low chair by the side of the little couch he occupied. As he said this she put her hand up and rested her brow upon it, covering her eyes by this means.

" Going away? you too!" she said, softly; "though I have known so little of you, I can't help feeling very sorry that you should think of going away. I detest these dissolutions," she continued, suddenly rising and walking away to the window.

"Dissolutions?" he repeated, echoing her last word.

"Yes, dissolutions; here just as Walter Goring is coming home, you, the only man who has been much to him during these later years, talk of going away. Walter had a reason for going and trying to turn himself into a barbarian—a reason I appreciated; but now that he is coming back sound and quite recovered from all that sorrow and mortification—coming back as he thinks to a band of friends who will welcome him, and be about him as of old—*why* should you want to be off?"

She faced round as she asked it—fronted him fully in all that "beauty such as never woman wore."

CHAPTER XVII.

"NOXIOUS VAPOURS."

SHE fronted him in all her beauty, reproaching him for thinking of going away, and her doing so nearly sent all his magnanimous determinations to be noble and miserable to the winds. Then he reminded himself that it was on Goring's account that she objected to the scheme—on Goring's account entirely. " She's not one of those women who like to see men wear their hearts upon their sleeves abjectly," he thought; "she's not one to want to add any fellow to her train of worshippers—she's had too many of them—*that* isn't why she wants me to stay ; she thinks about me so little that she doesn't even see that I love her."

He was uncommonly blind, quite as blind as he gave her credit for being. She did see how things had gone with the handsome young artist. He had

made his state of mind quite clear to her, and she
was not ill disposed towards it. His passionate admiration for her, and the chivalrous feelings which
kept him back from fully avowing the same were
patent and pleasant to her. But she could not make
any further move in an encouraging direction. She
had appealed against his determination to go away,
and he had reiterated that determination. There
was an end to that, of course.

It was rather hard work to go back to mere common places immediately after the excitement into
which they had both been betrayed; but she had perfect tact, and managed it. She rang for lights, and
everyone knows how infallibly the strongest thread
of conversational interest is snapped by the entrance
of a servant, who disorganises the room, and
abolishes the light of heaven for the evening. By
the time the lamp was on the table and the blinds
were down Mrs. Walsh and Frank were quite themselves again, toned down to perfect safety for any
number of hours' solitary confinement together.

By-and-by Charlie came back from her drive, not
at all exhilarated by it, as those who had advised
it had hoped she would have been. Indeed it may
be questioned whether one ever is exhilarated by

a visit, after a lengthened absence, to old scenes and old acquaintances. When, after a period of separation, one goes back to, or meets, old *friends* the case is widely different; but friends are not plentifully scattered over any one's path. The majority of people with whom one meets are of that calibre that one doesn't much care whether one ever meets them again or not. Therefore, when they do turn up, either premeditately or unexpectedly, one is apt to feel them to be uncommonly depressing and burdensome.

On the most shallow pretext they will refer to old times. They will go and dig in the mouldy past, and resuscitate the most unpleasant memories. They will remind one of something, not so intolerable in itself perhaps, but that brings to mind something else that is more than intolerable. They will remark upon one's tenderest points—on the crow's-feet of the maiden lady, who knows her last chance is going, if not gone—on the grey hair that plentifully besprinkle the raven locks of a past young, Apollo—on the immutability of one's prospects, which are no better and no worse than when they met one last. They will enlarge upon the preposterous prognostications that had been formed in the by-gone

time for one, and sigh over the falsification of the
same. They will remind one that as one was then,
and is now, so one will in all probability ever be in
this world. They ruthlessly (and undesignedly,
which makes matters worse) brush away the little
bloom that is left, and knock down the few remaining illusions. One can but ask, "What is the
motive" of all the striving, and struggling, and
sorrow, and suspense which, passed through, leaves
one in precisely the same position as before ? Many
who read this passage on a gloomy afternoon in
November will ask themselves the same question.
Here I think is the answer.

Because the ordeal brings out the highest qualities, develops the noblest faculties. Patience, endurance, pluck, none of these can have fair play while
there is no opportunity for their displayal. The
circumstances which call forth these qualities are
not pleasant—if they were the qualities wouldn't be
called forth ; still they are as good and strengthening
as a dose of quinine or a dip in the sea when the
chill of October is on it. They brace. Life is fully
worth all we suffer in it, as we must all acknowledge,
when we remember that on going into partnership
in the great firm of Humanity, we put nothing in.

All that comes to us of joy or grief, of pain or pleasure, is clear gain. We paid no premium. The majority of howls against the all-pervading sorrow and sin of this fair world are born of the cup that inebriates without cheering, far more frequently than from sober conviction. There is unfortunately too much of those sad alliterative twins, but inveighing against them in neatly turned sentences, or in mellifluous verse, does little good.

There is a very bright side to life as well as the dark one which has been so well worked by poets and romancists. There is a great deal of literal, of moral, and of mental sunshine, abroad in this world, which art too often " renders " gloomily. Of course it " is not always May." What a bore May would be if it were ? But if we look for the light we can generally find it even in suicidal November—or dreary dark December. I have a perfect faith in change and alternatives. If one place is wearisome, go somewhere else. If one thing does not answer expectation, try another. Every one may not be able to avail themselves of the former piece of advice, but the latter is at the command of all from the highest to the humblest. Work is an unfailing panacea for every

evil. Work induces hope, and assists digestion.
It is those who are drunk with idleness, not those
who cannot pause to dally, who find the world so
dark, and life so drear.

The story is so nearly told, that I have allowed
myself this digression without compunction. Moreover, the matter of it is not utterly irrelevant to the
declared subject. Mrs. Fellowes came back from
her visit to old scenes and old familiar faces, considerably depressed, it was stated, as may be remembered a few pages back. This depression was
a natural consequence of certain conditions to
which the most prosperous mortal may be subjected. In the first place, the heat of the day and
the confinement to the house had physically weak-
ened her. In the second place, she had been compelled to sit for an hour in the society of a stupid
well-meaning man (Mr. Foster), and a couple of
women equally stupid, and perhaps not equally
well-meaning, who had no interest in common with
her present all-engrossing pursuit, and no knowledge whatever of the place where she dwelt, or the
people with whom she mixed. This in itself would
have been of no consequence; but it became important when she was committed to sit amongst

and converse with them for a time. It is impossible for mediocre women to talk other than foolishly or far too curiously on any social topics of which they are utterly ignorant. Mrs. Fellowes, senior, and Mrs. Foster were eminently mediocre — the word seemed to have been made for them. They asked irritating little questions about things that could not possibly concern them, and they reverted to the old days with suppressed lamentations, and to the future in subdued tones that betokened much doubt. Altogether, Charlie was conscious of her chin having lengthened itself a little when she left them. They had stolen over her like a fog—they, and the recollections of the past.

Nor were matters brightened a bit when she reached The Hurst—her old home—the sight of which made her think rather kindly of the man who had lost it, and gone to distraction for grief at that loss. Mr. and Mrs. Prescott were sitting in the library, Ellen sitting at the still open window with a little stand close to her on which stood a candle and a plate of peaches. Ellen looked like a peach herself. There was a bloom—a downy tender softness on her cheek still. Not a line on her sweet, pretty face. " Time tries all but

Ellen," Charlie thought, as she looked at her sister.

Her brother-in-law was far less pleasant to behold. Mr. Prescott was sitting with a magazine in his hand, holding it up behind a candle, the light of which was cast fully on his face. Charlie saw at a glance that the magazine was one of those for which Frank drew. Presently she discovered that Mr. Prescott was criticising one of Frank's drawings.

Mr. Prescott's canons of taste were by no means uncommon. He liked what it was safe to like; what had received the commendation of centuries, or at any rate of the preceding generation. He would go and stand close up against Raphael's cartoons till each limb of each figure seemed a monstrous deformity, and find them surpassingly beautiful. He would view a Turner from that special point from which it was nothing but a smudge, and declare it "glorious." But he could see no good in the work of any young man without a name.

He had no faith in aspirants. "Fulfilments, not promises, were the things," he was wont to say. The young men who were upsetting tradition, and painting things as they were, received no encourage-

ment from that liberal patron of art, Robert Prescott, Esq. He would have his walls covered, but it
should be with something that was ' by,' or at any
rate ' after,' somebody of old, who could never cast
a suspicion on Mr. Prescott's taste by failing prominently to succeed contemporaneously with himself. Need it be said that he took a particularly
hopeless view of his brother-in-law's future. On
the advent of every fresh magazine — or new
number, rather — bearing those now well-known
initials, " F. S. J," in the corner of the principal
illustration, Mr. Prescott would enquire of his wife
'' what the good of it all was ? " adding with a snarl
that " that brother of hers wouldn't gain either
fame or fortune by drawing croquet-mallets and
neat ancles." Ellen agreed with him, of course,
and sighed for half-a-second over Frank and his
perversity.

When Charlie came in the evening, Mr. Prescott
put the magazine down on the table before him, and
gave it a fierce little pat.

" It will be a long time before that brother of
yours is able to do even this sort of rubbish again ? "
he asked, addressing Charlie.

Charlie by way of reply took off her hat, and

held her curly hair out to its extreme length, to let them see how long it had grown again.

" I say that he won't be able to do any of this rubbish again for a long time," Mr. Prescott repeated.

" Do you think not? " Charlie replied, unconcernedly.

Mr. Prescott felt his gorge rising. If Frank had only declared himself to be in an evil case, Mr. Prescott felt that he could have forgiven much. He didn't know what he had to forgive exactly, but " much " sounded magnanimous and was marginal, and he was ready to forgive it. But while Frank —and Charlie for him—bore himself bravely, Mr. Prescott could neither forgive nor wish him well.

" I can tell him that when he finds his daubing a failure he needn't look to me to repeat that offer I made him before of a berth in the city," Mr. Prescott said, testily.

" I don't think he'll want it, Robert; and I'm certain he'll never apply to you for it," Charlie replied.

" How's he to do without it, if his ' artistic talent ' " (Mr. Prescott tried a sneer and couldn't lift his lip) "fails him ? I'm speaking seriously, of a thing that may very possibly occur."

"Pray Heaven it won't, any more than all the shares you hold in everything may come to smash. However, Frank and I have cast in our lots together; while one of us can work, the other won't want."

"Maudlin nonsense," Mr. Prescott snorted contemptuously; "sounds very well just now before you have 'wanted;' but I'd have you think, Charlie —I'd have you think."

"What about ? " she asked.

"What about? why about what is to become of you both; how you're to live and be clothed and lodged; fine talking and fraternal affection won't satisfy your tradesmen, I'm thinking."

"Ah, don't try to dishearten me, Robert," she cried.

"I'm not. I'm only putting things before you in a plain light; you're not a girl any longer, unfortunately."

"Rather 'fortunately,' since I am compelled to shift for myself," she interrupted, with a rising colour.

"Well, that's a matter of taste on your part; I

said 'unfortunately' because there is no longer a chance of your marrying comfortably and being provided for in a way that will ease your friends of all anxiety on your account."

She remembered the time at Brighton — the hints that she had even before then received about establishing herself. She could not quote the horrible experience of her married life to these people, so she only said :—

" Putting that out of the question altogether, have you any other unpleasant fact to put before me ? "

" No ; I was only going to say that that maudlin nonsense you were talking about Frank and you having cast in your lots together being all humbug, it would be well for you to think seriously of what you'll do in the event of his marrying. Why doesn't he propose to Mrs. Walsh ? "

If Mr. Prescott had asked why Frank did not propose to the Queen of Sheba, Mrs. Fellowes could not have been more astonished. She regarded Mrs. Walsh as apportioned indisputably to Walter Goring—if Walter Goring chose to take her.

" I really don't know. In the height of our ' maudlin nonsense ' we never question each other on such topics; besides, Frank would never ask a woman to sacrifice for him—she would lose her property if she married."

" How do you know? You're very much mistaken."

"Ellen said so this morning."

"I'm sure I thought you said so, Robert," Ellen put in deprecatingly.

" I said I should make it a condition of my widow's marrying again, and that Walsh was a fool for not having done so. Of course you made a mistake; you never do comprehend if a fact and a suggestion are set before you at the same time."

"Well, it's no consequence," Ellen said, blandly; "take a peach. Mrs. Walsh is sure to marry Mr. Goring, so what does it matter whether she loses her picture or not. I remember once I thought that he'd have proposed to you, Charlie."

"Really—when?" Charlie asked; then a pang of annoyance caused her to add, "considering that I was engaged the second time I saw him and married the last, your reasons for thinking so must be very sound."

" Ah, but it was the *first* time you saw him—how

many years ago it seems. Gracious! *how* you're aged, and altered, and——"

"Dear Ellen, how exactly the same *you* are," Charlie replied, rising and putting on her hat. " I must go back now; Frank won't care to be late, and he'll want to see me before he goes to bed. We're off to town to-morrow, you know; so I shall not see you again."

So with a general embrace, the pleasant evening at The Hurst came to an end, and Charlie went back to Mrs. Walsh's, and when she arrived there was found to be not at all exhilarated by her drive and visits.

There was no opportunity of repeating a word of this conversation to Frank that night. Indeed, she felt no desire to do so. It had been very unimportant in reality, so far as she knew. All it was worth, in fact, was the further insight it had afforded her into a character of which she had known quite enough before. She determined to keep it till she was quite cool, and then recount it to Frank and make him laugh. As a study from real life, it might not be utterly valueless to them both.

The next morning Frank's arm was pronounced fit to travel, and Mrs. Walsh lost her guests, and

Deneham its choicest gossip. Frank and his sister went back to the semi-detached house in the secluded road, and Mrs. Walsh found Deneham duller than ever.

The talk about the old familiar topics had touched some long silent strings, and caused her to long to be free of that old world again ; to be once more within ear-shot of the jargon with which she had sometimes declared herself to be bored while Ralph lived. These are interests that can never be dropped entirely when once one has had a large share in them, and the wives of men who are eminent or earnest in any branch of art have a far larger share in their more æsthetic interests than outsiders imagine. The wife hears the best passages when they first drip from the pen ; she sees the favourable review, and points it out to him before anyone else thinks of looking for it; she is his guiding star in all matters of costume, and indeed in all that is good and at the same time feminine in his book, or most correct in modern costume in his pictures. After the never-ceasing excitement of such a life, it is almost impossible for a woman to settle down contentedly to a career of middle-class nothingness. Mrs. Walsh tasted blood in conversing with Frank

St. John. She hungered and thirsted for more when
he was withdrawn, and there was no one left with
whom she could go on conversing in a similar
manner.

"I was never meant to live an idle, albeit godly,
life down in the country," she said to herself,
laughing and shaking her head, after thinking long
and earnestly about these and sundry other things
the night of her guests' departure. "I wonder if
it's to be my fate to be seized with restlessness
now, and like the Paradise bird, never to find a
resting-place? I can't go on living here—of that
I'm sure. I should die of myself in a few months.
What a horrible vacuum agreeable people leave, to
be sure—in that Mr. St. John would see the law
of compensation at work again. He ought to do
something brilliant with that power of his. He's
one of the men who would be disheartened by
prudent recommendations to plod, but who might
be incited to do something splendid by one who
understood him. The painting and the poetry of
that 'Guinevere' are equally good; if he had
only learnt drawing before he did it, it would
have been superb; as it is, in the cant phrase,
it's full of promise, and shows that he will take

s 2

a foremost place amongst modern painters. How
proud—

She checked her reflections by rising up abruptly
as she recalled the fixed determination she had read
in his eyes not to speak the love that lived in them.
He had adored her too openly the first day—the
day they drove to Goring Place — for his after
scruples, whatever they might be founded upon, to
be justifiable. " Pythias won't interfere with the
bird notoriously winged by Damon," she thought
scornfully. " I daresay Walter is conceited enough
to believe that no amount of his indifference is
capable of curing me, and possibly has breathed
this belief into his friend's ears; if it wasn't that,
what *could* have come over the man ? "

What will the "only love" theorists think of all
this ?   That it is untrue to nature? or that I
viciously choose to depict a bad type of woman ?
Either supposition is equally incorrect, as any one
will find who can contrive to extract the truth from
the best women whom it is his happiness to know.
If Walter Goring had come home before this
meeting with Frank, Mrs. Walsh would never have
wavered ; but Walter Goring had not done so, and
Mrs. Walsh was conscious of wavering considerably.

Frank had stood a far better chance with the beautiful widow than he had imagined even in the maddest moments of his delirium.

It must be acknowledged that the long-contemplated tour through the western counties proved a mistake. They began to feel dull at Dawlish before they had been there two days. Then they moved to a village at some little distance inland, and hired the ponies according to programme, and regularly for the first three days of going out upon them, got wet through. Charlie had repeated that conversation which has been already detailed, which she had had with Robert Prescott; and from the moment of her doing so Frank grew more restless and gloomy than she had ever seen him before. He thought now, that had he only known this before he left Deneham, he would not have left Deneham in doubt; but after having behaved in the "idiotically undecided way I did when she said she was sorry I thought of going away, can't go back or write : it would look like an afterthought, and she wouldn't stand that ; the game's gone. Goring, as usual, will have the luck."

By way of improving his own spirits and rendering himself agreeable to Charlie, Frank took to discussing the possibility that was so odious to them both very freely about this juncture. "Probably we shall not see Goring when he first arrives; naturally he will go straight away to Deneham," he would say; and Charlie, though she did not think it at all natural that Goring should so conduct himself, was compelled to agree, because she had not the spirit to differ.

Dull as they found it — mistake though their riding tour was—they stayed away from London till the beginning of November, partly because Charlie dreaded the interval that must elapse between their going home and Walter Goring's return. But at the beginning of November they were compelled to go back in order to answer certain professional calls that were made upon them.

Once since leaving Deneham Charlie had written a sort of note of recognition for services rendered and kindnesses received to Mrs. Walsh, and Mrs. Walsh had replied to it civilly and briefly, and then the correspondence had ended. But they heard from Ellen that the widow was still down at her cottage, but that she had—such was the report—determined to give it up after the next quarter.

" Sharp measures," Frank growled. " Of course she won't want the cottage when she has Goring Place. But she's shaking off her old shell betimes."

The time was drawing very near for Walter's return. The housekeeper at Goring Place reorganized her staff, and the gardeners made frantic efforts to get the grounds into such order before the master's return as should induce that gentleman to believe that they had never been neglected. Mrs. Walsh robbed her own conservatory of the best flowers for the adornment of the room that had been Daisy's, in order that Walter might feel that neither he nor the dead Daisy were forgotten when he came home. The steward wanted to have something like a triumphal arch erected, and something like a procession of the tenantry and villagers formed to welcome back the Squire. But this Mrs. Walsh—to whom the steward confided his desires—negatived strongly. " I am sure Mr. Goring would hate it," she said; " consider, it will be his first visit to the old place since his cousin's death, and he was very fond. I know Mr. Goring so well that I may venture to say that he will be far better pleased to be received as quietly as possible." The steward

assented to her amendment quietly enough while
in her presence, but he went away and grumbled
at her interference. "She's a proud one, she is,"
he said to the select many to whom he had confided
his triumphal-arch hopes; "when she's married to
the master we shall have to mind what we're about,
or my lady will have us out in no time."

Up in town amongst those with whom we have
to do, there was equal excitement. The long-looked-
for had come. Frank found the announcement of
Walter's being in London awaiting him in a note at
his club one evening, and Frank rushed home with
the tidings.

"Goring is home!" he exclaimed.

"Oh, is he," Charlie replied. "I am sure you're
very glad."

"And are you not very glad, Charlie dear?"

Frank asked it very seriously. The sudden light
which had flashed all over his sister's face when he
told her that Goring was home, proved to him
plainly that Goring was very much to Charlie; so
much, indeed, that Goring's marriage with Mrs.
Walsh would be as bitter a misery to Charlie as it
would be to himself. Could that silly little Ellen
have been speaking the truth, when she said that

they were always unlucky? "I've had my share of ill-luck, surely," he thought dejectedly; "but this will be the worst of all; and I might have won her that night, if I hadn't been an ass and believed Ellen's gossip."

When Frank asked, "And are you not glad, Charlie dear?" Charlie replied: "I hardly know; it's two years and a half since I saw him—he may have forgotten *me* now!"

Frank laughed. "Have it your own way; I suppose it gives women pleasure to nurse such imaginative unpleasantnesses, or they wouldn't do it. Why on earth should he have forgotten you? Or how on earth could he, when he always mentions you in his letters to me, and I always mention you in my letters to him?"

"You never told me either fact, Frank," she said in a slightly injured tone; but the news though late was very welcome.

From that hour till the hour of seeing Walter Goring, young Mrs. Fellowes lived in a mental maze, and was conscious of it, and only quite alive to the fact of its being just as well not to make it patent to her brother that she was doing so. She was very impatient and very anxious. She was well aware that they had been very sympathetic to one another. She knew that Walter had taken a great deal of pleasure in her society, even when he was engaged to the younger, prettier, more exciting Daisy—even when that wonderfully beautiful Mrs. Walsh was attainable. But she also knew very well that a man may take a great deal of pleasure in the society of a woman who likes, admires, and appreciates him, without any feeling stronger than friendship reigning in his breast the while. She knew that he may be sympathetic, and that the very openness with which he makes manifest that he is so, is no poor proof of his being nothing more. She was very impatient to see him ; but very doubtful whether that sight would bring more to her than confirmation strong that she had sighed for that moon who smiled on so many brooks, and that the stars were unpropitious.

The best panacea for impatience—for every form of mental ill, indeed—is work. It is utterly impossible to be down-hearted when you are striving to be as coherent, amusing, or engrossing as it is in you to be on paper. If Mariana in the South had only been fortunate enough to get upon the staff of some of the magazines of the day, she would have ceased to be

so very weary. She could not have cared so much
about his coming while she was making copy; and
respite from wretched reflection is a great good
gained. Charlie believed in this all-potent panacea,
and worked a good many hours that day. Laboured
through some pages of Chaucer, at Frank's instiga-
tion at first, and then read him for love of those
subtle, delicate, quaint conceits—those turns of expression which can but enrich the vocabulary of the
most careless reader: read the " Faëry Queen " with
a gleam of understanding, thanks to Frank; and so
managed to pass the time away that necessarily intervened between that note of return being sounded,
and Walter's coming to them, without falling a victim to that sick prostration of soul which is the
common lot of the woman who fondly loves the man
who is coming to her—and to her rival.

She had been out a good deal since her return to
town. The visiting had come about gradually.
Frank had a good many friends, and was a very
good-looking man. The natural result of this combination was, that he was invited out a great deal;
and as he would not go without his sister, she doffed
her deep widow's weeds and went out with him.
Moreover, she was sought on her own account, as

being not alone a pretty, fascinating woman, but as
the author of a book that had succeeded, and that
augured well for her future success.   And she
revelled in these recognitions of what she had done,
and of what she was expected to do, and went forward, as was her wont, gladly, to meet any hand
held out to her in honest, unpatronising kindness.
She went once more, in fact, into the society of
which she had had glimpses in the Walshes' house
long ago, but, as was natural, on a very different
footing.

Altogether it had been a happy time.   The friendship that exists between a brother and sister is as
fine and thorough a one as can be formed between
any brace of human beings.   It is untainted by the
jealousies and misgivings which assail the subtler
union between husband and wife.   It is stronger than
any possible bond between sisters, and warmer than
the friendship of man.   And the best of it is, that if it
was cemented in childhood, however it may be in
seeming, nothing can destroy it in fact.   In boy-
hood's scrapes and manhood's troubles a sister is
sure to be a sympathetic confidante, though she may
be sorry enough for the matter confided; while for
the girl, a brother is the best, the only ally.

Frank and Charlie were friends after this pattern. She was proud of him—proud of his handsome face, and his debonaire bearing; proud of his popularity with women, of his invariable success with them, at the same time that his frank manliness made him well reputed amongst men. She was proud of his talent too; of the ease with which he was winning his spurs in two fields of art. In short, she was proud of him altogether, and especially proud of his pride in her.

She got more fun out of society when he was with her. Those hours that one spends on London staircases, or gasping in the doorway with a ghastly smile ready prepared to let off at your hostess and impress her with the fact of your being there and liking it when she is good enough to glance at you, those hours are all their length occasionally, when you have no sympathetic child of misfortune near to give back smile for smile. But when her brother was with her, Charlie was sure to get all that could be got out of the gathering. They were both very quick to see, as became artists; their correspondence was perfect, and their memories were good. On the whole they owed a good deal to society.

It happened on the day after Walter Goring

came home that they were going to an at-home at
a house familiarly known as the " Menagerie."
Walter Goring had called on them the night of his
arrival, but they were out and missed him. However, he left a note stating that he had met the
husband of the lady who was " at home " on the following night, at his club, and that he had pledged
himself to go to the Menagerie, where he hoped to
meet them.

When night came, Charlie, who had succeeded in
keeping apparently quiet during the day, gave up
the attempt, and got away to her own room " to
dress," she said. " What do you want to be hours
dressing for ? " her brother asked—he was finishing
a drawing on wood—and thought it "would be quite
soon enough if they got to Mrs. Drayton's at eleven."
As a rule, Charlie thought so too; but Walter
Goring might go and come away again before that;
she could not stand it.

" Oh, Frank, let me go at ten—do ! Mrs. Drayton says we're always late, and I don't want her to
think me affected about it."

" Who cares what she thinks ? No; wait for
me, Charlie dear."

" Not till eleven, Frank; I *can't.*"

"Why can't you?" he asked, wonderingly, looking up at her as she stood playing with the door-handle.

"I have nothing to do but dress, and when I'm dressed I think it odious to sit at home ever so long with bare shoulders and flowers in my hair."

"You needn't bare your shoulders or put flowers in your hair. I think you look nicer when you do neither," Frank replied; after the manner of men, he had some weak theory about simplicity and beauty unadorned.

"Let us compromise then," she said, laughing; "I'll meet you half way—half-past ten—will you go then?"

"Yes, I'll go then," he said; and then Charlie got away without further enquiries as to the cause for hurrying being made of her.

At half-past ten they reached Mrs. Drayton's, and had the satisfaction of finding themselves amongst the earliest. "This is very lively and pleasant," Frank whispered to his sister as he followed her up to the reception-room; "there's a thin sound flowing through the doorway that warns me that those of my fellow-creatures already assembled are conscious of feeling hideously conspicuous. This is your doing, Charlie; you wanted to come in with the lamps."

"*Never* mind," Charlie pleaded; "we can go the sooner."

There was the half-guilty look on the faces of those already there when Charlie and Frank came in, of being very clearly outlived, and also of feeling very glad that some others had come to share the sensation. The centre of the room was a barren waste, and the sides were but delicately fringed. A noble-minded girl was taking off her gloves towards the piano, and the hostess was wildly introducing people who did not want to be introduced. "So glad you're come," she exclaimed, holding out her hand to Frank. "Mr. Goring, the author of that delightful book on California, has promised to come in; and you've been there, haven't you? You can talk over your different experiences." Frank tried hard to look as·if he saw the humour of this happy speech being made to the artist of the book eulogised, when Charlie laughed about it afterwards, but he did not quite succeed someway or other.

Time dragged on; the rooms filled and over-flowed on to the staircase, but still the author of

that delightful work on California did not make
his appearance. "He has gone down to the place,
to see Mrs. Walsh," she thought sometimes; and
when she could banish that worst dread another
assailed her. "When he comes I shall be lost in
the crowd, and he won't see me; or I shall be
fastened upon by some bore, and he will be too
polite to drive him away."

At last the floor seemed to surge up to the
ceiling and the ceiling to come down to the floor,
and the faces around her grew indistinct, and their
voices sounded far away, and her heart thumped
audibly, as Walter Goring came in and saw her and
made straight for her at once, with the old look
in his eyes as he bent down to speak to her, with
the old warmth in the hand which she put hers
into so gladly, with the old tone in the voice that
said :—

"The sight of you makes me realise that I'm at
home again ; nothing else could have done it.
Where's Frank ? "

"Here, somewhere in the room," she replied, and
she trembled a little as she spoke. Two or three
people standing near to them scented a flirtation
immediately with the acuteness that marks the by-

standing mind. They did not know that it was long past that stage with one of them at least, if not with both.

He took her hand and placed it on his arm. "Let us get out of this; it's much cooler and clearer outside on the staircase; besides, some one is going to play, and I agree with Keats, 'Heard melodies are sweet, but those unheard are sweeter.'"

They made their way out into a comparatively quiet spot, and then she, finding that she could not stand steady any longer, sat down on the top stair, and a few who were near to them moved farther off judiciously.

"You look as you did the first time I saw you at Mrs. Walsh's," he said, bending down; "have you forgotten it?"

"No. I thought you would have gone down to Mrs. Walsh's at once."

"I shall go soon. I shall be glad to see her, and she'll be glad to see me; but there's no hurry about it. Long ago it might have been different, but somehow it wasn't different; now I perfectly understand. You remember the 'Knight of Toggenburg?'"

"Yes; what of it?"

"He sat down in the damp and died when she told him, 'Knight, a sister's quiet love gives my heart to thee.' I'm not going to die under the knowledge that my dearest old friend can give me no more, Charlie."

The words, the words she had longed to hear for so long a time, were on his lips almost, but at the moment Mrs. Drayton came up with a little red-faced man, who looked like one smile.

"My dear Mrs. Fellowes," the hostess began, " do let me introduce Mr. Moore to you;" then, in a whisper, "a remarkably clever young man—the author of an admirable work on 'Noxious Vapours.' I knew you'd like to know him."

What banes people are who won't let their guests find bliss according to their lights, especially when those lights lead them into sequestered nooks on staircases.

The talented author of "Noxious Vapours" was a tremendous bore to poor Charlie; but so Ana-creon or Sidney Smith would have been at the moment. Mrs. Drayton had carried Mr. Goring back with her, however; so Charlie had nothing for it but to endure the man of science and his smiles. "He looked as if he had been buttered," she said afterwards to her brother; "'Noxious Vapours' is without exception the most odious specimen of learnedom I've seen yet."

It happened, unfortunately, that "Noxious Vapours" thought kinder things of the young novelist than she did of him. He was one of those hapless men who never know when a woman is bored; and who clever though they are, never know how to avoid boring her. So he held her in the leash of his conversation till there was a move made to go down and have champagne cup and ices. Then Walter Goring went back to her, and somehow or other Mr. Moore, the talented author of "Noxious Vapours," saw through his own dazzling smiles that he was not wanted. And when Charlie left the Menagerie that night she was as happy as even an animal with a lot to eat and nothing on its mind can be. She was marvellously happy for a human being—with a happiness that stood every chance of lasting, for she felt that she was forgiven that first false marriage vow; her sharp, weary duty-time had been accepted as partial expiation. She had lived down the consequences of her first mistake, and was to be rewarded for a certain struggle, to endure the consequences of that mistake—a struggle which she

had made unceasingly, though she had been sometimes worsted—a struggle during which she had
humbled herself very much, and suffered very much,
and thought and repented very much—a struggle
during the continuance of which she had learnt that
the means do not justify the end, and that though
" there is a Providence that shapes our ends, rough-
hew them as we will," that we must not hew them
carelessly and rely on luck making all things straight
for us. She was rewarded for that struggle after
long years by being asked to marry a man who
loved her, and whom she loved. As she came down
to her carriage that night, leaning on the arm of
another than her brother for the first time for many
months, she felt that the clouds had cleared away
from her life, and that the stars which were shining
above did not make the sky half so bright as did the
love Walter Goring was throwing over it make her
future.

So the end came in a crowd, after all. No, not
the end, the beginning. We romance writers err
wofully in this, that we drop the lives of our young
people generally just when they are richest in promise. The " end " had not come to Walter and
Charlie when they pledged themselves to each other,

any more than it had to Mrs. Walsh when she heard of that pledging.   "I loved your husband very much from the hour he came to me with his first disappointment in literature," she said to Charlie some time afterwards, "and I love him still very dearly: but Frank would have put him out of my head, even if you had not put me out of Walter's."

That picture of Frank's had a mission, un-doubtedly!

THE END.

BRADBURY, EVANS, AND CO., PRINTERS, WHITEFRIARS.